Careful What You Wish For

Careful What You Wish For

A Novel

Anne Katheryn Hawley

Enjoy!
Anne Katheryn Hawley

A very fine
publisher,
if I do say so
myself...

Conundrum
Books
and
Music

conundrumbooksandmusic.com

ISBN: 978-0-9964370-0-4

Library of Congress Control Number: 2015909522

Printed in the United States of America

This is a work of fiction. Names, characters, places, and incidents either are the product of the author's imagination or are used ficticiously, and any resemblance to actual persons, living or dead, businesses, companies, events, or locales is entirely coincidental.

I dedicate this to my husband, Jim, for all of his support, encouragement, and enthusiasm as I read each developing chapter to him. He remains my biggest fan, as I do his.

Special thanks to Andy LePere of Kensho Studios in Traverse City, Michigan for his amazing and creative cover photography, and to Megan Kiehle, who modeled beautifully and gracefully for this demanding underwater photo shoot!

Conundrum*:*

A riddle whose answer is a pun;

A question or problem having only a conjectural answer;

An intricate or delicate problem.

7

Careful What You Wish For

Prologue

Meggie sat at her make-up table, resentfully getting ready for work. She suddenly noticed a lost eyelash resting on her cheek, and reached up to brush it away. She stopped short and thought to herself,

When did I stop wishing on eyelashes?

So instead of brushing it away, she gently wiped with her index finger and held the fateful lash balanced on the tip. She closed her eyes tightly, made a desperate wish, and forcefully blew it off.

Present Day

"I've got good news ... and bad news ... Which do you want first?"

"Oh for Pete's sake, give me the good news first."

Meggie could feel the irritation overtake her as Mark came in through the kitchen door, letting the screen door snap shut with a sharp bang behind him. That irritation came through in her tone as she spoke without even looking up from unloading the dishwasher.

"Mel's pregnant. The bad news is that we don't know who the father is."

Meggie stopped what she was doing and turned to look at her husband skeptically.

"How do you know she's pregnant?"

"It's kinda obvious. Her belly is looking awfully round, and her teats, or whatever you call them, are getting puffy-looking."

"Well *sacrebleu*! Neither of those things is *good* news, Mark." (Meggie would only swear in French-this meant *damn*!)

Mel, short for the God-awful name, Mellow Yellow, which Mark had insisted on calling the poor dog, was their pure-bred Golden Retriever. He was absolutely sure that by christening her such, she would not end up being a hyperactive nut-case animal like their last dog, which happened to be a Jack Russell Terrier creatively named Jack-in-the-Box.

They had felt forced to find another home for Jack when his incessant yapping and jumping up and down drove them halfway insane. So now they had Mel, whose nickname Meggie could live with. They had paid a fortune for her, and the plan had been to breed her, keep the pick of the litter, and make up for their financial investment by selling the rest of the puppies.

Meggie had told Mark a million times that when Mel was in heat to keep her in the house, and only take her out on a leash. But nooooo … he had just opened the door like always and let her out to prowl around like some puberty-stricken teenager. So now she was knocked up. Great. Just great.

"These things do happen," he said with a smug look on his face.

"It wouldn't have happened if you'd just listened to me and not been too lazy to take her out and walk her!"

"Why is it *my* fault? *You* could have taken her out for a walk just as easily as me."

"*I* have to go out and *work* while you're at home all day! Besides, I do walk her on a leash when she's in heat. This *is* your fault, Mark … and it's as easily as *I*, not as easily as *me*." Although Meggie had never attended college, being an avid and voracious reader had given her an elevated command of the English language. She found a certain degree of self-righteous satisfaction in correcting Mark's grammatical errors, though he almost always ignored her corrections.

"So what do you want me to do about it? Should I take her somewhere to get her an abortion?"

"Don't be such an ass," as she resumed putting dishes away. "The one thing you will have to do is to build a dog pen where she can have her puppies and then we can contain them …"

She paused, and then turned to look at him. "Why don't you help me empty the dishwasher?"

"I would, but I really need a shower … I'm drenched."

Mark's t-shirt had wet rings around the neck and each armpit, and sweat was dripping off the tip of his nose. He wiped it away and turned to make his way up to the bathroom. That annoyed her too. He took such good care of himself. He was obsessed with running. He spent almost an hour every morning out on these country roads. She had to admit though, he was in great shape. He could eat whatever he wanted, and as much as he wanted, and never seemed to gain an ounce. Meggie, on the other hand, didn't have *time* to devote to working out, and had to watch everything she put into her mouth to avoid gaining weight. It was *not* fair.

She replaced the clean dishes with the few dirty ones piled in the sink, then pulled the dishwasher door shut.

Meggie turned to look out the window over the sink. Mel was nowhere in sight. She went to the door and opened it to find the dog lying on the stoop. She went out and Mel lifted her head, tongue hanging out and tail thump-thump-thumping against the side of the doorframe.

Meggie sat on the step and scratched behind Mel's petal-soft ears.

"Good Girl … you a good, good girl Melly. Melly gonna be a momma? Huh, girl? You gonna be a momma? Yes … you a gooood girl …" She spoke in that childish tone and pattern of speech people tend to take on when speaking to their pets.

Sure enough, Mel's mammaries were swollen and her belly was definitely getting quite round.

Meggie sighed and looked out over their land. Ten beautiful acres, most of it heavily treed. They had neighbors, but also plenty of elbow room. They had not wanted to spoil the open feeling by putting up a fence for Mel, so they had opted for an invisible fence, which pretty much kept Mel in, but unfortunately, and apparently, hadn't kept at least *one* of the male dogs in the neighborhood *out*.

It really irked her that other people were not as responsible about their pets as she was. She wondered which one of the neighborhood dogs might be the father, and what the puppies would look like.

The grass definitely needed mowing. Why couldn't Mark notice these things and take care of them before she had to say something?

Pour le Dieu … (For God's sake …)

Later that evening, Mark and Meggie sat out on the screened porch, eating a dinner of creamy baked brie, sliced Granny Smith apples, and a loaf of crispy French bread. Meggie was drinking Chardonnay. Mark preferred Merlot, and had almost polished off the bottle.

"Hey Meggie … I'm sorry I let Mel out like that. I wasn't really thinking …" He reached out to take her hand in his, massaging it while looking at her with his famous half-smile, brows raised … the look of contrition with a touch of mischief. This look tended to get him out of trouble, especially when coupled with an unsolicited massage.

Meggie closed her eyes, allowing the soft manipulation of her hand, and tried not to smile. When she opened her eyes again, his expression had not changed. He could *still* get her with that look. She smiled at him, taking her right hand away and replacing it with the left. "Here … now do this one …" she murmured.

"I'll do your feet and back later … after I clean up the kitchen. My penance."

"I wish you wouldn't make it sound like punishment, but I'll take you up on it!"

"You got it. Bring your wine upstairs and take a long, relaxing bath. I'll be up when I finish the dishes. And don't worry, Meg, putting my hands on you is no punishment whatsoever!"

Meggie leaned forward and kissed Mark lightly on the lips, then stood, picked up her glass and walked to the door,

saying with a smile, "You don't have to tell me twice …"
as she disappeared through it.

Meggie thoroughly enjoyed luxuriating in her claw-foot
bathtub. She filled it almost to the top before stepping into
it, and then slowly eased into a reclined position, wincing
slightly at the heat. She splashed the very hot water up onto
her forearms and shoulders to get her skin used to the
temperature before lowering them under the surface. She
stopped when the water level reached her neck, took a deep
breath, and sunk until her face and head were submerged.
Her hair floated like seaweed at the edge of the ocean. She
felt like Medusa. Her ears popped slightly and she became
aware of the drone of the underwater silence.

Little bubbles escaped from her nose as she opened her
eyes to watch them follow each other to the surface in little
lines.

She continued to hold her breath as a distant memory filled
her mind … a recurring memory that she was never quite
sure had simply been a dream, or had indeed happened to
her …

Twenty-three Years Earlier

She couldn't swim. At only six years of age, she felt ashamed and embarrassed about this shortcoming.

Especially now.

Meggie had been invited to spend the day at China Lake! Kimmy Buckley, who spent the summers with her grandmother, was a year older than Meggie, but the two played together often; that is, when her grandmother allowed it. She only lived the next street over, but seemed to think that Meggie and her mother were from "the other side of the tracks". At least she acted that way, according to Meggie's mom.

Meggie was more than thrilled to be graced with the invitation. Opportunities like this didn't present themselves to her all that often, and so far, this had been one incredibly hot, muggy, and unbearable August. But today she was going to the lake!

Meggie's mom had the breakfast shift at Denny's, so Meggie dug her bathing suit out of the pile of clothing on the closet floor, scoffed down a bowl of cheerios, grabbed a towel from the bathroom, and ran over to Kimmy's grandmother's house.

She was worried that they would leave without her—that they hadn't really meant it or something—which is why she ran all the way. But there they were, waiting patiently for her.

They piled into Kimmy's grandmother's rusty Buick, and off they went.

The first disaster of the day happened after only about 30 minutes of the hour-long drive from Bangor to Winslow.

Meggie got carsick.

Kimmy's grandmother did not even attempt to hide her disgust as she cleaned up the stomach-acid and cheerio-remnant mess at the first gas-station-slash-convenience-store they'd come to. Thank goodness they sold cleaning supplies.

"I'm sorry," Meggie whispered to the back of the headrest as Kimmy's grandmother *whumpffed* back into the driver's seat.

Kimmy hung over the passenger seat, holding her nose and giggling as she said to Meggie, "That was GROSS!"

"Turn around and sit down Kimmy! Meggie, do you think you can make it the rest of the way?" asked Kimmy's grandmother with exasperation.

The interior of the car now stunk of vomit and Mr. Clean. Kimmy's grandmother was forced to open all the windows which allowed the oppressive heat to blow into the car. It felt more like a hairdryer than a pleasant wind, but it did help to eliminate the stench.

As they finally neared the China Lake area, the aroma of balsam fir tinged the air—a very pleasant change.

The upchuck episode was forgotten as they turned onto the wood-chipped drive, and the dark green, soft-needled branches swept fleetingly into the still open windows as they passed.

"We're here! We're here!" shouted Kimmy excitedly.

Kimmy's grandmother looked into the rear-view mirror to smile at Meggie. She now felt badly for the way she had treated the poor girl for something that she couldn't have helped.

"Meggie? Are you feeling better?" she asked.

"Yes Ma'am." Meggie had been well-trained to respect her elders.

"Do you like to swim?"

"Yes Ma'am!" Meggie was starting to anticipate jumping into the cool water, and temporarily forgot her plight about not being able to swim.

The rustic cottage at the end of the driveway they had pulled into was very secluded, but with a nice waterfront about fifty feet from the structure. It belonged to Kimmy's grandmother's bosom buddy, Ms. Toni, as she was introduced. Ms. Toni and Kimmy's grandmother exchanged greetings in bird-chirp-like twitters, and then quickly began discussing their favorite soap opera …

"Can you believe what Nikki has done now?"

"Well, Victor pushed her to it!"

The Young and the Restless would be starting shortly, and both women were anxious to get inside so as not to miss a detail.

As they made their way into the cottage, Ms. Toni reminded Kimmy that the water toys were in the boathouse. Kimmy's grandmother instructed them to *stay near the dock*, and then the two women disappeared to martinis and their "stories".

The sights, sounds and smells filled Meggie's senses. This was a whole other world from the one she knew. The water lapping at the pebble-strewn beach was crystal-clear.

The lake was surrounded by dense evergreen trees, which created a privacy and peacefulness that made Meggie think that *maybe* Ms. Toni owned the *entire* lake. The contrast of the vibrantly verdant trees against the brilliant azure sky, punctuated by impossibly white, fluffy clouds was so dazzling that it made Meggie's eyes water. She inhaled the heavy pine scent and somehow believed that this must be what heaven was like.

"Come on!" cried Kimmy with a degree of both excitement and impatience as she ran toward the old, weathered boathouse.

Meggie followed, her flip-flops flap-flapping against the bottoms of her feet as she, too, ran toward the shore.

She stopped at the water's edge, suddenly considering just how deep this beckoning water might be.

The water at the first foot or two of shoreline was so transparent that Meggie could see every rock at the bottom, but then it seemed to get abruptly very dark blue, which left the depth to question.

Kimmy dragged out a little blow-up boat that not only was still inflated, but did not appear to have any holes in it either.

"Let's swim first, and then take this boat out for a spin!" *Everything* Kimmy said was an exclamation.

Meggie kicked up some of the sparkling water with her feet, losing one of her flip-flops in the process.

"I'll get it!" shouted Kimmy as she ran and jumped full-barrel into the chilly water.

"AAAAAHHHH!" she screeched as she came to the surface. "It's FREEZING! Jump in, Meggie!" Kimmy laughed and splashed at Meggie.

Holding her ineffectual hands up in front of her to ward off the onslaught of the surprisingly cold water, she managed to blurt out,

"But I can't swim!"

"What do you mean, you can't swim? How old *are* you, anyway?"

"I'm six."

"Well *I* learned when I was FOUR! I learned at the pool!"

The community pool was only a block from Meggie's house. Every summer they offered swimming lessons for which they charged a dime per lesson.

 After that, in order to be able to swim freely in the pool, a "tadpole test" had to be passed for which they also charged a dime.

The dime for this necessity of life had never been offered, nor had Meggie ever dared to ask for. Being raised by a single mom who struggled to make ends meet as a waitress didn't afford luxuries like *life survival skills*. Besides, Meggie's mom was much too preoccupied by the parade of boyfriends that never seemed to end.

So if and when Meggie had visited the community pool, it was only to sit at the shallow end, dangling her feet, or maybe to wade in up to her waist. Ten cents seemed to be the magic number. They even charged a dime to use the bathrooms, with little slot machines on the doors which wouldn't open without the deposit. Meggie remembered the one time she had actually begged a passerby for the funds to use the toilet, being a number two emergency situation. She had been quite amused by the graffiti written on the inside of the door:

Here I sit, broken-hearted, paid a dime, and only farted.

But the swimming lessons were never an option, so here she was … standing helplessly at the shoreline.

Kimmy continued to swim, jump, splash, and stand on her hands under water with her spindly white legs and feet splayed at the surface. She was laughing with utter delight as Meggie jealously and longingly looked on.

After awhile, Kimmy got bored with enjoying the water by herself, and exclaimed, "Let's take the boat out!"

Meggie was reluctant, because of both the frigidity of the lake, and her fear of what could be lurking out there in the deep, indigo water.

"Don't be a silly-willy! We can just sit in the boat and use our feet to paddle around! It will be *FUN*!"
Kimmy could be quite persuasive in a demanding sort of way.

So Kimmy and Meggie arranged themselves in the little boat, which was just big enough for them to sit, back-to-back, with their legs dangling into the water from each end.

They floated around in the shallow end, where Meggie could still see the rocks and pebbles. This made her feel safe. But then Kimmy began to kick her feet and propel them to where they coasted above the mysterious darker water. Meggie clung to the soft plastic sides of the boat and leaned into Kimmy's back. The warm sun felt good on her goose-bumped skin, especially in contrast with the temperature-induced numbness in her calves.

Just as they passed the outermost end of the sun-bleached dock, Kimmy suddenly and *very* unexpectedly pushed herself out of the little blow-up boat with an exaggerated *SPLASH*.

Although Meggie was pretty scrawny, her weight on the one side instantly tipped the plastic vessel and quickly dumped her into the deep water. Before she went under, the icy coldness of it forced her to gasp in a deep, shocked breath.

She did not even make an *attempt* to swim. Meggie simply descended to the bottom, cheeks puffed out like a blowfish of some kind. Down ... down ... down she went, and as she was sinking, she gazed up at the surface of the water above her submerged body.

The sunlight glimmering off the small, undulating waves was like some beautiful optical illusion of light, and Meggie was mesmerized.

Her skinny little bum hit some slick, hard rocks at the bottom, and Meggie could no longer hold her breath. At first, the bubbles escaped through her nose as she attempted to retain oxygen, but her diaphragm, needing to expel the built-up carbon dioxide, forced the air out of her in a rush. That very same diaphragm then expanded involuntarily, meaning to pull in a fresh dose of air, but instead, the icy water was what was sucked into little Meggie's lungs.

The sharp and intense pain of it lasted a millisecond. That was all. Just a millisecond. And then Meggie was strangely and suddenly filled with a sense of calm that she had never experienced in her young life. She felt like she was in the arms of the most loving, protective and strong mother ... or father ... or *some*thing. Meggie was physically and emotionally *comfortable* in a way that defied description. She simply ... *felt*. And it was ... *good*.

Meggie looked again toward the surface, and watched as the lights that had been dancing on the waves above seemed to converge and cast a beam of very warm, soft light which was directed right toward her. She basked in this soft warmth, and the feeling that no harm would come to her—*ever*.

The cold, bony arms that abruptly encircled her waist were an unwelcome interruption. Meggie suddenly felt herself being pulled *up—up—up* in jerky movements. The next thing she knew, she was heaved out of the water and onto the splintery wood of the warm dock. She began to cough and retch almost violently as her lungs desperately fought for oxygen.

As the wracking began to subside, Meggie became aware of the young girl at her side. She could make out that the girl was a teenager, maybe fifteen or sixteen years old. She was extraordinarily pale, with freckles spattered over her face and shoulders. Her short, curly, and *very* red hair threw off a shower of the lake water as she shook her head and wiped at her eyes. "Are you okay?" she asked a bewildered Meggie, who had begun to cry, curling herself into a ball on the hard surface.

In the distance, Meggie could hear the piercing sound of Kimmy's screams, and then the confused exclamations of Kimmy's grandmother and Ms. Toni as they responded to the ruckus.

Meggie half-raised her head to respond to her rescuer, but when she looked back up, the girl was gone. Simply *gone*.

Instead, the anxious faces of Kimmy's grandmother and Ms. Toni filled the space and blocked out the sun, as one of them frantically shook Meggie's shoulders, shouting in a high-pitched shriek,
"MEGGIE! MEGGIE!"

When they came to the realization that Meggie was indeed alive and breathing, Kimmy's grandmother took the waif-like girl into her arms and began to weep. "You scared us, little Meggie," she croaked through her tears.

Present Day

To this day, Meggie believed from the depths of her soul that her rescuer had been her guardian angel. Neither Kimmy's grandmother, nor Ms. Toni, and not even Kimmy herself had seen the red-haired girl. Where had she come from? Where had she disappeared to? *Someone* had pulled Meggie from the depths of the lake that day … *the red-haired girl!* She was Meggie's guardian angel. Meggie just knew it.

Sometimes Meggie had wondered why she'd even been saved. From what she remembered, she would not have minded one bit if nobody had ever rescued her. It was because of this memory that Meggie did not fear death. Not that she would go out looking for it, but somehow this incident made her sure that there was something far better on the other side, and that death was not the unpleasant and formidable experience that many believed it to be.

Meggie had not been raised in a church. The only times that her mom would make her put on a dress and drag her to some church service was when she happened to be dating someone who felt that Meggie needed this kind of exposure to God. Meggie still didn't know too much about the Man, but she thought about Him, and speculated—*a lot*. She kept a Bible by her bedside, and sometimes would pick it up, praying—almost pleading, "Teach me something I need to learn today." She would then open it randomly, hoping that some incredibly poignant and instructional words of wisdom pertaining to her current crisis, whatever that might be at any given moment, would be revealed.

Most often it didn't work out that way, but every once in a blue moon, a certain passage might bring her some comfort. Reading the Good Book was work—hard work—and it most often provided Meggie with more *questions* than answers.

Meggie bolted up out of the water, gasping to fill her lungs with sweet oxygen as water splashed over the edges of the tub.

She sat for a few minutes, as the memory of the day at the lake faded into the recesses of her mind. She decided to do some self-maintenance. She shaved her legs and underarms, which was long overdue, and then trimmed her toenails which were now soft and easy to cut after being in the tub for so long. When she was done, she put on clean underwear and one of Mark's t-shirts, and climbed into bed.

While waiting for Mark to come up and fulfill his promise, she began to read her current book, *Worth More Dead*.

She kept a stack of pending recommended books to read close at hand on her nightstand. She was thrilled that this novel had been recommended, and was enjoying it immensely. Reading a good book was probably her greatest enjoyment. Meggie never watched TV. It wasn't long though, with a glass or two of wine in her system, before her eyelids became heavy, and she started to doze off.

She was on the cusp of sleep, but just awake enough to be aware when Mark finally came in and climbed into bed next to her.

"You still gonna do my feet ...?" she asked groggily.

"Oh ... sorry Meggie ... but can I give you a rain check? I'm kinda beat ..."

"... Yeah, sure, whatever ..." she said, disappointment being the last emotion she felt before succumbing to subconsciousness.

****

"Here come old flat-top, he come—grooovin' up slowly, he got—joojoo eyeballs, he one—"

"Sounds good, Meggie. You missed your calling."

Meggie quickly turned pink as she realized that she was no longer alone in the office early on this promising morning, but smiled in greeting to her fellow agent, Greta.

Meggie had an eager buyer! A bonafide and more importantly *pre-qualified* buyer! Meggie worked as a real estate agent who specialized in finding just the right homes for buyers who were new to the area … job transfers and the like. She was good at it, particularly because she actually *listened* and heard what a buyer said they were looking for. Meggie also tried hard to stick to the buyer's price ceiling, unlike many other agents, which she knew was a reason that potential buyers would seek a different agent. Occasionally, Meggie would take a listing of her own, but didn't really like some of the baggage that came along with that, like dreary *open houses*, and spending her *own* money for advertising. Half the time, another agent would be involved anyway, so she'd have to split her commission, and that was *after* her broker took his generous cut. It just wasn't worth it to her.

Meggie had probably been in just about every single home at one time or another in the Traverse City area. This town was like a little slice of paradise. When most people thought of Michigan, Detroit would come to mind.

This was not the most flattering image for a state that kept its natural beauty and *intensely* gorgeous shoreline a fairly well-kept secret. Downstaters were aware of the jewel that Northern Michigan was, but apparently the rest of the world wasn't in on the secret. This was just fine with Meggie. In her opinion it helped preserve the very beauty that she was so in love with. Human beings, especially in large numbers, always seem to spoil their surroundings. Why *is* that?

Meggie had been born and raised in the equally beautiful State of Maine, but moved to Traverse City after meeting Mark at a Tae Kwon Do competition in Boston ... way back when. *Waaay* back when ... when Meggie used to be *almost* as obsessed with her physique as Mark still was. She had trained in the art of Tae Kwon Do, mostly for self-defense purposes, but had been good enough to place in some competitions. But no more. She had allowed herself to get soft. Not fat, mind you, but soft.

When she met Mark, he was in the process of opening his very own Tae Kwon Do studio just outside of Traverse City, in a charmingly countrified community called Interlochen. His excitement about his plan had been contagious. That, along with his handsome face and endearing smile, had easily captivated Meggie. Their very brief long-distance relationship had quickly turned into a long-term living together situation when Meggie had agreed to make the move to Northern Michigan as both his business and his life partner. They had married within a year.

The business did pretty well for the first five years, as had their marriage. Both Meggie and Mark taught martial arts classes at the studio, and Mark handled the nuts and bolts side of the endeavor.

Mark had received a good sum of money when, tragically, his parents died in a car wreck. Mark was 21 years old at the time, and a student at MSU. His parents had been Christmas shopping at a downstate mall, heading back toward Saginaw, where they had lived their entire lives. A large buck darted out onto Interstate 75 in front of the couple … and that was that.

From that point, it took Mark another three years of being a "senior" at MSU, changing his major multiple times and floundering in his classes, until he realized that all he really wanted to do was martial arts. So he quit college without graduating.

He took the money that had been sitting in an account just waiting to be spent, and moved to the Old Mission Peninsula, where he bought the farmhouse in which he and Meggie now resided. He became obsessed with Tae Kwon Do, and quickly became a top competitor, locally and nationally.

Mark had used the remainder of his bank account when, at the age of 27, he opened his studio after purchasing and renovating an old barn on M-31. Meggie had been thrilled to be a part of something so exciting, and especially with good-looking and athletic Mark, the love of her life!

She often wondered what happened. Why and how she got so tired of it all.

Real estate had always held a fascination for Meggie. Maybe it was because when she was growing up she had never had an actual "home". She and her mother had skipped around from one crappy, cheap apartment to another, until "the event" which sent Meggie out on her own in the cold, cruel world at the tender age of 16 going on 17.

It had seemed to be a natural transition for Meggie to acquire her Real Estate license when Mark's business began to slow three years ago. The intent had been for it to merely supplement their income, but as time went on, Meggie found that she preferred selling houses over the rigors and bruises of teaching the brutal and physically demanding Tae Kwon Do classes.

So many of the homes in the Traverse City area were gorgeous, restored Victorians, just the type of house Meggie had always dreamed of living in. There were also plenty of pretty lakefront cottages, and beautiful farmhouses on rolling acreage.

Meggie thoroughly enjoyed walking through them, admiring the original woodwork, high ceilings, tall windows and gleaming wood floors. She truly would get *just* as excited about a house as her buyers, which often helped turn it into a sale.

At this point, Meggie brought more money into the marriage than Mark's slowly failing Tae Kwon Do business. She didn't particularly like that fact. Thank goodness the house was paid for! But she didn't particularly relish the idea that she was getting "soft" either. Today; however, this unpleasant detail was unimportant, There was a *sale* in the air, and Meggie could almost *taste* it ...

"He got hair—down—tooo his knees. Got to be a joker he just do what he please ..." Meggie resumed singing the song she couldn't get out of her head, but sort of under her breath now that Greta was here. The printer spat out the last listing that Meggie planned to show her client today. She picked up the pile, tapped them on the desk to straighten them out, and placed them in a folder, then told Greta, "Wish me luck!" as she sashayed out the door.

****

A commission from a home sale was definitely a reason to celebrate. Meggie was always the one who did the planning for a night out. She wished that Mark would take it upon himself to surprise her one evening, even leaving "hints" like cutting out from the newspaper a fun-looking event, or a special that was being offered at one of the local restaurants, and then taping it to the fridge. She did more than just give hints, but Mark never picked up the ball. Meggie actually would periodically *ask* Mark to take the initiative and plan something nice for the two of them *before* they were old and gray. Mark would respond by saying, "But I never know what you want to do!" Then Meggie would reply, "Take a look at the fridge door before you open it! I couldn't make it any easier for you, Mark."

Meggie felt as if waiting for her husband to take her out on a "date" was like "Waiting for Godot". It simply never seemed to occur to Mark to plan a date night out with his wife. And so it was always just left up to Meggie. Somehow, this made "date planning" seem like another one of her many "jobs" robbing her of the joy that a continued *courtship* might have added to their marriage. Oh, the honeymoon was over, that was for sure. The only upside of this was that she could always plan to go where *she* wanted to go.

One of her favorite places in town was an elegantly rustic French "bistro" called *Amical*. It was kind of expensive, but well worth it. Not only was the food absolutely amazing, and artistically presented, but the atmosphere was warm and cozy, with romantic lighting, exposed brick walls, wood floors, and colorful oil paintings in beautiful frames adorning the walls

Being a Friday night, Meggie called to make reservations. After confirming a table for two at 7pm, Meggie decided to try out her French speaking skills, and said, "Merci … Au revoir!" The hostess taking the reservation replied with a hesitant, "Ummm … excuse me?"

"Oh, I'm just thanking you and saying goodbye in French …" Meggie was now embarrassed that maybe she hadn't said it right, but the hostess laughed and said, "Oh yeah! Bonjour!"

Meggie smiled to herself. She had been trying to learn how to speak French for many years using home-study computer courses, and still only knew a few phrases. She had memorized some swear words, and things that she might want to say when she didn't want the person to whom she was speaking *know* what she was saying. Meggie felt that cussing was "ugly", and therefore preferred using the French equivalents, which somehow sounded "pretty" despite their meaning.

Meggie then called the studio. Mark had recently taken over teaching an after-school class for ages twelve to seventeen. He was totally bummed about having to let his only remaining assistant go, but Mark couldn't justify paying someone when he himself had the time to teach the class. Especially with business being so slow. Class times were now limited to Tuesday and Thursday evenings, these Monday-Wednesday-Friday after school classes, and three back-to-back classes on Saturday mornings. Needless to say, Mark had a good bit of free time on his hands, but he filled most of this with running, biking, and surfing the net. No wonder he was so darned buff!

"Studio Han-Du-Se. How can I help you?" Mark used his professional, authoritative voice when he answered the phone at the studio. It was tinged with a sound of hopefulness ... hope that maybe he had a prospective student on the line, or better yet, a school that wanted to add a martial arts program.

Poor Mark! Meggie wasn't sure why his studio hadn't remained successful. At times she felt sorry for him, yet at other times she was angered by the failure. At the moment it was the former.

"Hi Sweetie! Guess what?"

"Hey Meg! What's up?"

"We're going to *Amical* tonight—my treat! I made a sale!"

"Cool Meggie ... that's really cool ..." Mark loved to eat—anytime, anywhere, though his favorite place in town was *Boone's*, where he could get a hefty hunk of tasty, tender beef. But he knew how much Meggie loved *Amical*, and added enthusiastically, "So what time?"

"I made our reservations for seven. I'll go ahead and pick out something for you to wear."

"Sounds good, Honey. And congratulations! Which house did they buy?"

"The gorgeous three-story on Eighth Street. I had a feeling they'd pick that one … It's the one I would have picked!"

"Meggie … we're *not* moving …"

Mark was well aware that Meggie would just jump at the chance to move into one of those Victorians in town. She wanted to be where the action was, not that there was a whole heck of a lot of action in Traverse City. But she adored downtown, and enjoyed the paved bike trails. And she *loved* the homes in that area. Mark preferred the open expanse of the big, old farmhouse — the bucolic peacefulness of his own land …

He also preferred riding his bike along Peninsula Drive, or M-37, where he could *really* ride. Cruising the bike trails at Meggie's sight-seeing pace was not really his favorite thing to do …

"I know, Mark. I *know*. I didn't say *anything* about moving."

"Yeah, but I know what you're thinking."

"It may surprise you to know this Mark, but you don't *always* know what I'm thinking."

"So what are you thinking then?"

"I'm in a *very* celebratory mood. *Now* do you know what I'm thinking?"

"Well, heck! Let's hurry up and go eat!"

Meggie laughed.

"See you when you get home, Sweetie. And don't be late!"

****

Mark was late. Not too late that they'd miss their reservation, but late enough that he had to rush to take his shower and get dressed while Meggie impatiently waited at the bottom of the stairs, shouting up at intervals, "Come *on*, Mark, we're gonna be *late!*"

It didn't take much to get Meggie "out of the mood", and here she was, planning a nice, romantic evening. *Maudit!* (another French word for *Damn!*) She and Mark still had an active sex life, but it had become so … *perfunctory*. They had a tendency to cling together afterward, like two lost children. Every once in awhile Meggie would try to create something magical … something that she believed sex was *supposed* to be. She would light candles, put on some soft jazz, and dress the part in a sexy, though classy negligee. But Mark seemed almost … *uncomfortable* in that scenario, and was always ready to just get to the point. He never said anything, and always tried to play the part appropriately, but Meggie could sense that his heart wasn't in it … that he was somehow just going through the motions to please her. She wished that this knowledge alone of his wanting to please her could be enough, but it wasn't. Meggie never stopped trying, although her unrequited attempts were becoming farther and fewer in between.

Well, tonight Mark was off the hook. Meggie no longer *felt* like going to the trouble to make it nice. Another dull night of … perfunctory. And that was *only* if Mark got his butt down here so they could make their reservation!

As Mark clomped down the stairs in his stiff, rarely worn wingtips, Meggie thrust his jacket at him as she attempted to hide her frustration. Why did he have to be late for everything and anything Meggie planned?

"*Sacrebleu*, Mark. Let's GO!"

"I don't know why you always insist that I wear these shoes, Meg. They're pretty uncomfortable."

"If you'd wear them more often you'd break them in faster and they'd soften up. Are you saying that you'd prefer to wear your old, stinky sneakers?"

"They'd sure be a lot more comfortable."

Meggie just shook her head as she led the way out the front door. If Mark had things his way, he'd wear sweats and sneakers everywhere. He was no fashionista, *that* was for sure. It annoyed Meggie that he didn't seem to want to trouble himself to dress nicely for her. It pissed her off even more that he happened to look great in *whatever* he wore. Meggie had to work at it, especially lately. She bit her tongue. She knew that she became very irritable when she was hungry, and right now, she was *starved*. Besides, Mark had been a good boy and dressed in the outfit she'd laid out for him. He looked great.

****

"I'll have a Bellinitini, please." Meggie smiled up at the handsome young waiter as she ordered her drink.

"I'll have the darkest beer you've got on draft." added Mark.

"Oh, and I think we'll start with the sesame seared tuna appetizer ..."

A sudden commotion at the front of the restaurant caused Mark, Meggie and the waiter to look toward the door. Two young women had burst in like a blast of wind, laughing loudly as they entered and surveying the room as though they were walking onto a stage. They were both very pretty, but one was exceptionally striking. All heads seemed to turn as the hostess led them back to their table.

As they passed Meggie and Mark's table, the bombshell appeared to stumble slightly, her hand finding Mark's broad shoulder to steady herself. Mark quickly looked up, the astonished expression on his face, quick blush and huge smile making it clear that this was a welcome intrusion on his personal space. The girl giggled, squeezed his shoulder, smiled brightly back at him, saying, "Sorry 'bout that!" as she tossed her mane of incredibly glossy black hair over her shoulder.

Apparently, she's already had a drink or two, thought Meggie bitterly as she too, smiled up at the beauty, though it was more of a grimace.

"It's okay." Meggie said, as Mark simultaneously, and a little too loudly babbled, "No problem whatsoever … perfectly alright …" as he still smiled stupidly.

The two young women took their seats at the table behind and just to Meggie's right. Mark watched with his mouth hanging open, oblivious to Meggie's sudden wrath.

"Mark, shut your mouth for crying out loud, you look like some kind of love-struck idiot."

"Don't be ridiculous, Meg." Mark shot back, refocusing his attention on the menu in front of him.

The air still whispered the soft, clean and spicy scent of the girl—it was like it had settled into the air at Mark and Meggie's table. Mark inhaled deeply, while Meggie looked at him with daggers in her eyes.

Their drinks and appetizer arrived. Meggie took a long swig of her Bellinitini as soon as it was set on the table. Her stomach was so empty that she could actually feel the chilled, raspberry flavored liquor glide smoothly down her esophagus and into her grumbling tummy.

After placing their orders for dinner, consisting of Beer-braised Beef Brisket for Mark, and Nut-encrusted Walleye with Beurre-Blanc sauce for Meg, they dug into their appetizer.

"Holy Cow! I think I just cleaned out my brain!" exclaimed Mark with watery eyes after dipping the tender AHI into a nice dollop of Wasabi.

"Take it easy on the green stuff, Mark—it's got horseradish in it, I think." Meggie was already reaching for her third piece.

"You take it easy on the appetizer, Meg. You're acting like you haven't eaten in days."

"It almost feels that way, and geez, I can't help myself—this practically melts in your mouth—*delicious*!" as she stuffed another tuna-laden sesame cracker into her mouth.

She was starting to feel better already, and downed the rest of her drink. She caught the waiter's eye, lifted and pointed at her empty glass, and he buzzed off to get her another.

Mark was looking around the room, his glance repetitively landing on something, or *someone* just beyond Meggie's right shoulder.

"What are you looking at Mark?" she asked snidely.

Mark turned to focus on Meggie, completely ignoring her tone.

"The artwork, Meg … look at it … don't you think it's kind of … rudimentary?"

Meggie rolled her eyes. She knew damned well what, or at *whom* he was looking, but decided to let it go and play along. She looked around at the walls to consider the paintings.

"Well … I suppose they are a little amateurish-looking. But so what? They look good in here. And I think the focus is supposed to be more on the use of color."

They only look good because of the frames ..."

"Could *you* do better?"

"Probably!" and then he laughed.

Meggie laughed too until she noticed Mark's eyes drifting once again over to the object just behind her right shoulder. She turned around quickly and caught the hair-commercial-model attempting to avert the dazzling smile she had been beaming in Mark's direction, and gracing it instead upon her stupid friend sitting across from her. As Meggie turned back around, the two girls broke into a silly giggle. Meg's face began to get hot as she watched Mark grin sheepishly with a slight shake of his head, as if he was in on some private joke with these two wenches at Meggie's expense.

Just then, Meggie's second drink arrived, with a promise from the waiter that their dinners were on their way.

"Well, you may as well bring me another drink, then ..." said Meg to the waiter as she lifted her martini glass to her lips, draining half of it in one swallow.

"Uh ... yeah ... coming right up." replied the young man a little uncomfortably.

"I'll take another beer while you're at it." added Mark.

The tension at their table was palpable. Mark and Meggie glared at each other for a second or two.

"Meggie—those drinks have got to cost close to ten bucks a pop—geez!" he whispered harshly.

"For heaven's sake, Mark—don't be such a *cheapskate!*"

This was said with enough volume to make sure that the occupants at the table to the right and behind Meg could hear every word.

She continued loudly, "Besides, *I'm* the one paying for this meal … when is the last time *you* brought home a paycheck?"

This time it was Mark's turn to blush crimson as he struggled to maintain composure. His eyes darted once again you-know-where, but only for an instant, and then he smiled at Meggie and reached for her hand.

"I'm sorry, Honey. You're right—we're here to celebrate your sale. Drink as much as you want."

"I will!" as she drained the glass. "Man! Those are good—more like fruit juice than a drink-drink." But Meggie was most definitely feeling the effects of the liquor, and unfortunately, it was bringing out the worst in her. Of course, Mark's thoughtless behavior was contributing to that. Even so, she was *not* going to let this night out be spoiled by Mark's ridiculous flirtations. It wasn't like this was anything new.

Their meals arrived, along with their next round, and they got down to the business at hand.

The food was outstanding—it was easy for them to become totally absorbed in the senses of taste and smell as they devoured their meals.

Suddenly the two from the table behind Meggie got up to leave. Apparently, they were only having drinks and *salads*—of course.

Again, the glossy-haired girl's spicy-sexy scent permeated the air as she *swooshed* by, and she actually had the audacity to repeat her performance with a stumble and a hand landing on Mark's shoulder. She laughed with a sound that to Meggie's ears was like a hyena, and then ducked her head toward Mark's so that her long hair brushed across his face as she said, "So sorry—I can't believe that happened *again!*"

Mark gazed up at her and couldn't have smiled a bigger smile, even if someone had placed forceps in the corners of his mouth.

"My pleasure ..." he said.

Meggie just stared at him as her stomach churned.

"What?" Mark asked Meggie as the jingling laughter of the girls faded with their noisy exit.

Meggie continued to stare, stone-faced, at her husband.

"Come on, Meg—you know, you just can't stand it when another woman in the room looks *better* than you!"

Meggie was both stunned and stung by the cruel and ungallant words that came from her husband's mouth. She swallowed hard and struggled to hold back the tears that this insult provoked.

Looking down at her plate, stirring the remainder of vegetables around with her fork, she managed to stutter out a shaky response, "Mark, every woman wants to be the most beautiful in her husband's eyes. You constantly make it obvious that *I'm not* by your incessant flirtations and ogling ... how on earth do you think that makes me feel?" Mark was silenced by his own realization of just what it was he had said to his sweet wife.

Meggie continued, but would not look at Mark as she spoke, "Frankly, there is almost always someone in the room that looks better than me. I would just prefer *not* to know that you've noticed. You make me feel like you'd rather be with someone else," as a tear spilled down her cheek.

"Awwww ... shit, Meggie. I didn't mean to say that."

"Mark, only a *boy* tries to make his girl jealous of other women. A *gentleman* makes other women jealous of his girl."

Mark didn't quite know how to respond. His silence was almost as bad as his flirtation.

Meggie knew that it had been a Freudian slip, and that Mark had meant it alright, and now she was getting mad again.

"Yes, Mark. You did mean it. *Tu es completement debile.*" (*You are a complete moron.*)

"Alright already. Enough with the French cussing." Mark said, but with a contrite tone. He had absolutely no idea what Meggie said when she spoke French, regardless of how often he heard a word or phrase. And he had heard *that* one a lot.

They finished their meal in silence, paid the bill, and went home.

****

Meggie went straight upstairs to take a bath when they arrived back home, while Mark settled in the living room to watch his sports, another obsession for him. Though Meggie appreciated Mark's physique, she also resented the time he devoted to working on it. And work it was. It had finally proven to be too tough for Meggie to keep up with herself. After her bath, she stood in front of the mirror, critically assessing her naked body. At times, Meggie would catch a fleeting look of disapproval from Mark when she was barely clothed, or completely bare, but it was always fleeting, so she was never sure. Maybe it was in her own mind due to her insecurities. Mark was never less than complimentary to her regarding her shape … everything about her, really. He was just so damned *stupid* sometimes when it came to other women. His behavior certainly added to Meggie's doubts as to Mark's sincerity. And it wasn't that she didn't trust him. He was a "look but don't touch" kind of guy. But it was his constant "looking" that made Meggie feel like she wasn't quite good enough. Mark did tell Meggie "I love you," just about every single day. Nothing in particular would prompt it, and it was said with such matter-of-factness. Sometimes he would ask her, "Have I told you that I love you today?" Meggie felt that one big reason for Mark's doing this was because of suddenly losing his parents, and not having the opportunity anymore to tell them he loved them, which truly broke her heart. But somehow, the constant repetition of the words had made them lose their meaning. It always sounded so rote when he said them. Kind of like the desensitization one experiences when exposed over and over to something or other.

Meggie reserved her "I love you" s for when she was actually *feeling* it.

She tried to observe herself objectively. She couldn't believe that she was almost thirty years old! Time flew—twenty-nine years GONE—just like that! Wouldn't it be nice if she could just jump into the clothes dryer for a few rounds, and come out wrinkle-free and a few sizes smaller – or tighter somehow? Her almost C-cup breasts already appeared to be droopy. They used to seem to stand at attention all on their own. Mark referred to them as "the girls". He would say, and sometimes at the most inopportune times, like when Meggie was cleaning house, or on her way out the door to meet a client, "Let me see the girls." It could be incredibly exasperating. She cupped her hands beneath them, lifting them ever-so-slightly—*There! That's better!* Her eyes drifted down to her belly. She had always had slim, boyish hips, and now that her mid-section had thickened, any curve that used to exist had somehow vanished. She turned to survey her backside. Her rear-end was most definitely the fat-magnet. Her startlingly white derrierre was dimpled with cellulite. *How disgusting! I am going to lose this fricking weight!* she thought angrily.

Meggie then pulled her hair out of the high ponytail that had held it out of the water during her bath. She was a natural strawberry blonde, and her thick hair was one of her best features, though she had gotten into the habit of twisting it into a messy bun at the nape of her neck and wore it that way most of the time. She made a mental comparison of her own locks to the thick, glossy mane of that shameless hussy at the restaurant, and found even her best feature to be lacking. *What on earth does Mark see in me anyway?* She asked herself miserably as the memory of her envy filled her up just as acutely as it had only a couple of hours ago. Was Mark right? Could she really not stand it when there was a prettier girl in the room?

There were many times when Meggie was no doubt the prettiest girl in the room. These were times when she felt the most confident and most comfortable coming out of her shell. But for some reason, she would always scan the room, and *did* become uncomfortable if there was competition. Why did she *do* that? Why did it matter? Maybe it was because she could always count on Mark to notice any and every good-looking woman, and did not seem capable of curbing his flirtation or his ogling. It was *his* fault that she was insecure. And he would always make it about her insecurity when she complained about the flirting—basically blaming her, and making her feel like something was wrong with *her* that his behavior bothered her! Was that true? Was something wrong with her?

Meggie leaned in toward the mirror to look more closely at her face. She had beautiful almond-shaped eyes, blue-green with goldish flecks, almost luminous. Her lashes were light-colored, but long. Mascara was a necessity. She made a mental note to use the stuff more regularly—it definitely brought out her eyes. She had full, pink lips, and a cute smile, though not perfect by any means. One of her front teeth slightly overlapped the other, but her smile was wide and warm. She practiced in the mirror, doing a sort of mock-laugh as though someone had just told her a funny joke. She suddenly remembered the perfect, much-too-white joker-grin of the girl in the restaurant. Maybe Meggie should look into getting a tooth-whitener of some kind? She could just bet that *that* girl used a whitener.

Meggie's nose was delicate and straight, with a fine spray of freckles just over the bridge.

She thought to herself, I *am* cute. I just need … a little work. So right then and there she made the commitment to some self-improvement.

****

"Have you noticed Mel throwing up lately?"

"Uhhh ... no ... have you?" asked Mark as he raised his coffee cup and eyed Meggie questioningly.

"Hmmm ..." she replied. "No, I haven't seen her throw up."

"Why on earth would you ask such a weird question?"

Meggie looked at him with exasperation.

"She's pregnant, Mark. Haven't you heard of *morning sickness*?"

Mark chuckled condescendingly, "Meg. I don't think that dogs get morning sickness."

They sat in silence as the morning sun dappled through the trees and onto Mark and Meg's disheveled morning-hair, each of them sipping their coffee, heavily laden with toffee syrup and hazelnut cream. Their morning coffee was more like a dessert, but it was a ritual they enjoyed and were addicted to.

Mel was at Meggie's feet, belly getting rounder by the day. She panted her pleasure with her drippy tongue hanging out as Meggie petted the pitiful, pregnant pooch.

"So ... have you put any thought into that pen I asked you to build? This will be—what? the third time I've had to—"

"Meggie! I'll *get* to it for crying out loud!"

"Yeah sure, Mark, but when? She's going to drop these puppies within the next few weeks. We have *got* to have a place not only for her to give birth, but where we can safely keep the puppies until they're old enough to give away! I honestly don't know what you do with all your time …"

"I *said* I would get to it."

"You've been saying that for almost three weeks."

Mark stared silently into the distance, blatantly ignoring Meggie.

She got up to take her coffee back inside. It was such a beautiful morning, and should have been a pleasant one, but now she felt so annoyed that all she wanted to do was to get away from Mark. Mel followed her to the door and watched as Meggie disappeared through it, tail thumping and tongue dripping onto the stone walkway.

Poor dog! thought Meggie. *How on earth would Mark know whether or not dogs get morning sickness?*

Meggie was irate that Mark hadn't been able to get a simple dog pen built by now. Everything, simply *everything* was a fight.

The proverbial "leaving the toilet seat up" was a very real source of stress for Meg. If she had asked Mark once, she had asked him a zillion times, "*Please* put the toilet seat down after you use it. And while you're at it, could you work on your aim?" It was so gross, especially at night, when Meggie would work her way in the dark to use the toilet, and end up sitting unexpectedly on the cold, pee-covered porcelain!

Mark would say, "Why do you get so upset over something that's really not a big deal?"

And Meggie would respond, "If it's a big deal to me, then it should be to you. And if you don't think it is such a big deal, then why don't you just *do it*?"

Round and round they'd go.

And it wasn't just about the toilet seat ... it was about putting an empty carton of milk back in the fridge instead of throwing it away ... it was about the overflowing garbage can and the constant "forgetting" to even take the garbage out ... it was about not noticing when the lawn needed to be cut ... it was about forgetting Meggie's birthday, or their anniversary ... it was about farting or belching at the dinner table as if manners were not necessary with his wife ... it was about ... Mark's *indifference* to Meggie's thoughts, feelings and complaints. He would roll his eyes and make the excuse that these things were so insignificant, so unimportant ... and *not* a big deal. Meggie just couldn't understand why, if these things weren't a big deal, Mark wouldn't just be thoughtful and humor Meggie. It was as if he *wanted* to provoke her, repeating the very behaviors that he knew drove her crazy. *Mon Dieu!* She was so easy to please ... why didn't Mark care enough to *try*?

She poured herself another cup of coffee, adding a very generous and deserved portion of syrup and cream, until the color was light caramel, and went to the kitchen door to glare out at Mark. Mel was still there at the stoop, waiting for her, and began wagging and drooling. Meggie wondered again about the morning sickness thing. She placed her hand over her own belly …what would it *feel* like to have a child growing in there?

****

Mark worried about his mortality. Meggie wasn't so sure that she knew how to be a mother. So they had decided early on in their relationship that they did not want children. Meggie blamed her own mother entirely for her deficiency in this area—after all, how could you learn parenting skills from someone who obviously wished that they weren't one? Or maybe Meggie was just scared. Mark never pushed the baby issue as he was perfectly happy only having himself to worry about. And Meggie never felt that urgency of a biological clock ticking. This world could be very, very cruel, as both Mark and Meggie had experienced—and besides, what was the point?

Meggie had pondered this question frequently-what's the point? Was there a heaven? And was God's *will* done there? If so, wouldn't all of our souls be nothing more than puppets in heaven? Meggie had memorized *The Lord's Prayer* when she was a child. Despite her mother's lack of faith, bordering on contempt of faith, Meggie had recited this prayer in her head every night when she went to bed.

But Meggie's analytical and doubtful mind had made her question even *The Lord's Prayer*. "Thy Kingdom come; Thy will be done; On earth as it is in heaven." Meggie just couldn't understand why God did not exert his will right here on earth, especially if he was going to do it in heaven anyway. There was so much pain and suffering … so many horrible abuses of innocents. Meggie herself had been a victim of horrendous abuse. And where was her guardian angel then? Sometimes Meggie felt foolish for believing in her, but she couldn't help it.

The *event* (which was more like a series of events leading up to the one that left her homeless at sixteen years of age) was a memory that Meggie both struggled to obliterate, and also had to struggle to remember. She had blocked out quite a bit of it, but remembered just enough to make her physically ill when her thoughts took her there.

She considered the way people prayed for God's interventions …Please, Lord, make Grandma better … Oh, God, please help me get this job … Our Father in heaven, please send me the love of my life … or, God, please grant us world peace.

So which was it? Could God intervene, or were we mere mortals left to our own devices in a world filled with evil? Did God give us all free will, and on top of that sinful natures, and then sit back to watch the show? If he *does* intervene, how does he pick and choose? And how is that fair? He certainly wasn't there for Meggie during her darkest days, despite her furtive, desperate prayers.

And yet … Meggie fiercely, almost frantically wanted to believe in a kind, benevolent, fatherly (or what she thought a father should be, having never had that experience) God who protected his children and *loved* them—no matter what!

Meggie knew there was an afterlife. Her guardian angel had saved her from drowning. The whole thing had been otherworldly … supernatural … spiritual. But where had that angel been when Larry, the devil himself, entered their lives with his sicko wickedness? Meggie's mother had been so consumed by keeping her boyfriend happy that she had turned a blind eye to the sexual abuse going on right under her nose.

She had not only failed miserably in protecting her only child, but had actually blamed her child for the perverse molestation committed by that creepy cretin. The man should have gone to jail for the atrocities he had forced upon a *child*. Once she left, Meggie had never looked back. What kind of mother would abandon her own young daughter in favor of a perverted predator?

If *Meggie* had a child of her own she would … she would … *what?*

Mark didn't want children. Neither did Meggie … or *did* she?

Who had made that decision, anyway? Her mind wandered back to when she and Mark first met—she had been *so* in love!

10 Years Earlier

Meggie normally did not take much notice of men, not even when they were good-looking. She was much too busy learning how to protect herself from them.

But this guy? There was *something* about him …

She had heard his name announced over the loudspeaker several times, and now made her way to whichever event he might be competing in to watch inconspicuously within the crowds.

Mark Simpson.

Good Lord—he was so cute! Meggie had never been affected by a guy in this way. She loved the way he was sculpted—strong, sleek, with no bulky show-off musculature. He was tall, and had a great posture. But he seemed humble at the same time that he seemed confident, which Meggie found very appealing. He seemed *kind* … a regular joe who had a ready smile for everyone, including his competitors. He took defeat with a winning attitude, though he had won many events. He was most definitely a gifted athlete, but without all the usual conceit. Meggie liked him—a lot—before she had even met him.

What Meggie didn't know was that Mark had taken notice of her as well.

Wow. This girl is *good*, Mark thought, and almost too cute to be doing this sort of thing. It was quite impressive to watch this delicate creature move with such determination. Her small frame belied the wiry strength that had placed her in several events.

Her shy demeanor took over after each time she competed, and she would quietly walk to the bench all by herself. She was like a little, fragile bird pretending to be a tiger.

Meggie McGregor.

He even liked her name.

As the afternoon wore on, Mark began noticing that Meggie was noticing him. She had flushed a vivid pink the first time he caught her eye, which had the effect of making his heart swell. Their glances graduated to smiles, until finally he approached her as the competitions came to a close.

"Great job today. I've been watching you, and you are deceptively *really* good—powerful kicks, and quick on your feet!"

"Thanks. Same to you, and congratulations on your wins!" She smiled at him and he instantly fell in love with her crooked smile and scrunched up, freckled nose.

"Are you hungry?" he asked.

"Ummm … why do you ask?"

Mark laughed and sheepishly replied, "I suppose that wasn't such a smooth way to ask you to go have dinner with me, was it?"

"I'd love to."

"That's great! I'm Mark."

"And I'm Meggie. So you really think I'm good?"

"I don't think—I *know*."

"Ha! I don't think you know either!" Meggie laughed.

"Ohhh … a wise guy, eh? Alright Ms. Meggie McGregor, let's go get some grub."

Meggie's heart leapt. He knew her name!

"I'll go grab my stuff, Mr. Simpson, and be right back." she said with a smile on her face and in her voice.

"I'll wait for you as long as it takes." he smiled back, making his own mental note that she also knew *his* name.

All the restaurants in the area were packed and on long waits, so Mark and Meggie picked up some BMTs at Subway and Meggie invited him to her place to eat. For some odd reason, she trusted him and felt comfortable with him. It was like for the first time in her life she was where she belonged, and with whom she belonged. Meggie had been living in Boston for a little over two years. It was a great town to "get lost" in, which was what Meggie had needed to do when she left, or rather, escaped home. To this day, Meggie did not know the extent or permanence of the damage she may have caused when she slammed a baseball bat into the side of Larry-the-monster's big, thick skull. For all she knew, he was permanently brain-damaged, or permanently dead. Meggie's mother had been screaming bloody murder, calling Meggie a slut, a whore … words that mothers shouldn't say to their daughters let alone screech them out so the whole world could hear. Meggie had frantically stuffed as many clothes as she could fit into a dirty pillowcase before blindly running out the door and the mile or so to reach the Greyhound Station. She bought a one-way ticket to the furthest place she could afford, which happened to be Boston, and never looked back. No, that's not true, she looked back over her shoulder in fear almost constantly for that first year. Now only if she heard a voice that sounded like her mother or Larry … or a police siren. Meggie had had the wherewithal to steal the money she knew that her mother kept hidden in a pair of boots in the closet, as her mother had tended to the brute's bloody brains. So, Meggie was a thief, and possibly even a murderess. This, and these wretched facts of her youth would *not* be the story of her life that she would tell Mark this evening. No … Meggie made up her mind as they ate their subs that she would keep her sordid past close to the vest, especially after listening to Mark for the past hour talk about his fairy tale childhood and amazing parents. Did families like this really exist? Meggie felt a mixture of envy and something else—maybe it was the way children feel when they watch fairy tales—hope—yes, maybe that was it, the hope that a better world really *did* exist. The kind of world in which parents loved and doted on their kids. The kind of world where families were *happy*. The kind of world Meggie barely dared to dream about, let alone believe in. Mark's stories about his mother's cooking, the family vacations, the time spent with his Dad, fishing, playing ball … Mark's being able to talk about anything and everything with his parents, and their intense interest in all Mark ever thought, said or did. It was like a dream childhood … an Ozzie and Harriet world. Meggie wanted that kind of world *so badly*, and here was someone who just might be able to give it to her! Meggie was not about to run him off with the ugly truth. So instead, she told him about the *one* happy memory that she did have. It was a memory that she clung to like a lifeline … It was a time when Meggie's Mom was in-between boyfriends, but rather than her usual dark, depressed and brooding no-boyfriend-personality-change, she was in one of her fast and loud-talking, hyperactive and insane energy, let's-have-fun personality changes. The latter was usually reserved for the men in her life, but it was always one identity or the other. This time, it was Meggie for once who benefitted from the hap-hap-happy mood her mother was in. They had loaded up the car with bathing suits, towels, a couple of large bowls and some wooden spoons for making sandcastles, and a lunch of peanut-butter sandwiches, potato chips and lemonade. They headed down to Bar Harbor and Mt. Desert Island. Meggie had never before seen anything as beautiful as this rugged and spectacular Maine coastline. The deep blue of the ocean, with swells that made the water seem very much alive and restless—the sheer vastness of it was staggering! Meggie and her Mom ate their simple lunch as the waves splashed up around their feet at Sand Beach. They threw their crusts up to the hovering seagulls, and laughed. The water was too cold to swim in, but the sun was warm and bright, and Meggie felt *loved*. They drove over the mountainous roads circling the picturesque island with the radio blaring and the windows rolled down. But the highlight of the day was when they stopped at a place called *Thunderhole*. It was truly the most amazing sight Meggie had ever seen, still true to this day. The rocky coast had somehow split, creating a corridor of granite walls, with a deep crevasse into which the massive ocean swells would pulse. As the powerful undertow pulled the water back out to sea, the combination of the two phenomena, along with the hole that was somehow created at the end of the stone corridor, caused the water to volcanically erupt after it got sucked into the hole, then hit the back granite wall. The sudden gushes of water spewed well above the walls of the corridor, and though pretty much contained, the cold spray would rain down in sheets, collaterally saturating the observers standing safely behind the sturdy rails of the observation deck. It felt dangerous and exciting. It seemed like Meggie and her Mom stood there and watched it for hours, totally mesmerized by Mother Nature's power and beauty. The experience, and the place itself, almost defied description, but Meggie must have done a pretty good job as she regaled Mark with her precious memory.

"Holy cow! I want to go there!" he exclaimed with the appropriate amount of awe.

"Have you never been to Maine?"

"No … my parents talked about going there, but we never did. We always seemed to go to either Traverse City, or the Upper Peninsula … or Mackinaw Island …"

"Well, it's never too late."

Mark suddenly went white, and his eyes got a funny look to them, like he had seen a ghost or something. His eyes got glassy-shiny, and as he attempted to speak, he choked up.

For a minute there, Meggie thought she was going to have to do the Heimlich Maneuver … "What's wrong?!"

"They're … gone. My family's gone."

Meggie could tell that Mark was struggling to maintain composure to keep from crying. At first, she was confused.

"Gone?"

Mark took a deep breath, looked down and began to wrap up the remainder of his sandwich.

"Yeah … they died in a car wreck. Six years ago."

"Oh God. Oh, Mark. I'm so sorry." She suddenly wanted to wrap her arms around him, but settled on putting her hands over his. Personal interaction was not one of her strengths, and even this small act was a stretch for her.

"It was a long time ago …" Mark said after squeezing Meggie's hands and then releasing them with a grateful, but sad kind of smile.

After this shocking revelation, and witnessing the pain that he evidently was still carrying after his tragic loss, Meggie didn't know where to take the conversation, but Mark began talking about his faith, and how it had carried him through the life-changing event and subsequent and bottomless void.

While on the one hand, Meggie didn't want to contradict the very thoughts that seemed to bring Mark comfort, she simply couldn't understand how God could be so cruel. How could he separate this exceptional family? Here she was, in a self-imposed exile from her own hateful, insane, and very much alive (as far as Meggie knew anyway) mother, while Mark's loving mother had been senselessly ripped away from him. Why? So Meggie kept her mouth shut and just listened. Mark apparently had an unwavering belief in God. A belief that he and his parents were saved by Jesus' sacrifice on the cross. A belief that his parents were now in heaven. And a trust that God knew what He was doing.

Did He? Meggie's mind was flooded with doubt, questions, ifs-ands-buts as the familiar platitudes, meant to soothe the broken heart, spilled from Mark in a way that just felt false. Like Mark was trying to convince *himself*—after all this time.

"They're in a better place. God always takes the good ones. I'll see them again one day, I know ..."

Later in Mark and Meggie's relationship, discussions revolving around God and faith would become more open, honest, lively and even argumentative—almost like debates. But for now, Meggie just quietly and solemnly agreed with everything Mark was saying.

How she wished she could have such simplicity of thought—such steadfast faith …

Mark continued,

"There's always a silver lining somewhere within the pain … you know, all that's come before has somehow led me to you, Miss Meg McGregor."

Finally—something that *made sense* to Meggie.

Present Day

Mark had a new student. And this guy was as good as Mark, if not better, in the art of Tae Kwon Do. He brought a life to the class that had been lacking. This new guy, Ryan, made Mark's challenging, yet boring class—*fun*. Ryan had a joke for every occasion. He did a great impersonation of Austin Powers aka Mike Meyers that often had the other students rolling with laughter. It didn't take long before Mark and Ryan became friends. So Mark invited Ryan over for dinner one evening.

Meggie was in the kitchen, totally pissed off that Mark had sprung this upon her. She did *not* feel like having company. And if Mark wanted to have a friend over for dinner, shouldn't *he* be doing the cooking for this meal? *Maudit*! And to top it off, the guy was fifteen minutes late already!

All of a sudden, there was a rap-rap-rap on the kitchen door. Meggie turned as a young, handsome, and very muscular fellow let himself in as though he owned the place. He walked right up to Meggie, his large brown eyes, a bit magnified by a fashionable pair of Buddy Holly glasses, never leaving her face. He reached out to grasp her hand in both of his.

"Good God." He said, as his steady gaze moved from her eyes, to her lips, and back up to her eyes.
"You're *gorgeous* …" He seemed dumbfounded by her apparent "beauty", and Meggie swallowed nervously, while inside she absolutely glowed from this unexpected

77

adoration. It had been awhile since she had been the recipient of such attention.

Before she could respond, Mark walked into the kitchen, oblivious of the exchange and the electrical charge in the room.

"Hey buddy! So I see you've met the wife …"

"Yeah! Sort of … but not officially." He then took Meggie's hand, raised it to his lips, and took a bow, and in an impeccable imitation of Austin Powers said, "Allow myself to introduce … uummm … myself!" and then immediately he went back into gentleman mode, " Ryan, your humble servant." Meggie pulled her hand away, laughed self-consciously, and said, "And I'm Meggie. Nice to meet you."

This evening was turning out to be not-so-bad after all …

"I apologize profusely for being late. I was unexpectedly detained by an officer of the law on my way over here.

"You're kidding!" exclaimed Mark. "What happened?"

"Well, you know how birds sort of congregate on telephone wires, right? So I came to a stoplight over there on Division. Some car behind me backfired, and those damned birds went nuts. They were all over the damned place – kind of like that Hitchcock movie, *The Birds*. One of'em slammed into my windshield and his wing got stuck in my windshield wiper!"

"Holy cow! Really?"

"Yeah, man. So I turned the wipers on to get rid of the thing."

"Did it work?"

"Hell yeah it worked. However, the car behind me happened to be a cop car. The bird flew off my windshield, bounced back and landed on his windshield, and got stuck in *his* wiper!"

"Oh my God!"

"The next thing I knew, the cop put on his flashing blue lights, then got out of his car, came to my window, and issued me a ticket!"

"You have got to be kidding!" said Mark incredulously.

"That's unbelievable." said Meggie. "What on earth did he give you a ticket for?"

Ryan hesitated briefly until he knew he had both Mark and Meggie's full, anticipatory attention.

"For flipping him the bird."

It took a second for the joke to sink in, but they all had quite a laugh. For Meggie, the ice was broken. She already felt that she'd known this guy forever.

The meal was utterly delightful. While Mark gave Ryan the "tour" of the house, Meggie changed plans. Instead of simply eating at the kitchen table without frills, she set the outdoor table festively with candles and their best dishes.

Somehow it made the everyday meal of hamburgers and fries a little more special. It was a beautiful evening, and they sat drinking wine and talking effortlessly until way after dark. Ryan had story after story to tell. He had been in the military and had traveled extensively. He seemed so worldly! Meggie was fascinated, and so was Mark.

Toward the end of Ryan's soliloquy, he suddenly realized how he had been monopolizing the conversation by talking incessantly about himself, not that Mark and Meggie had minded. He had actually been quite entertaining. So, he said,

"Well, enough about me!" and then leaned forward, looking expectantly at Mark and Meg, "What do *you* think about me?"

Once again, he had them laughing.

When Ryan left, he gave them each a warm hug. Was it Meggie's imagination, or was the hug he gave her very warm, very close, and a bit lingering? She wasn't sure, but if Mark noticed anything, he was hiding it well. He was quite obviously as enamored with Ryan as Meggie was.

****

Mark and Meggie had an ongoing competition. They played chess. It made sense, as the genesis of their relationship was based on competition. As time moved on, they played more rarely, but this stormy evening had left them without power, which meant no boobtube. The game didn't seem to bring its usual joy. Instead, there was an animosity in the air. They were having to work hard to even be nice to each other. Mark was winning *that* game, but not by much. He was, however, losing their ongoing match, as Meggie clearly had more wits.

"You know, Meggie, you've always been more analytical than me, which is what gives you the edge in games like this. I tend to see what's right in front of me rather than anticipating what might be lurking ahead."

"Like when you fail to see the mayonnaise you're looking for when it's sitting right there behind the empty milk carton you put back in the fridge?" Meggie asked snidely. "...And it's more analytical than *I*—not more analytical than *me*." she added for good measure.

9 Years Earlier

When Meggie stumbled upon Mark's "secret", hidden away in the corner of the attic space above the bedroom closet, there were many things she still didn't know about him. Details she was afraid to even ask him about. But this discovery was so strange—in a *Great Expectations' Miss Havisham* kind of way. The pile of Christmas presents, tattered and torn, yet still wrapped and remarkably intact considering their age and what they'd been through ... it reminded Meggie of the cobwebbed reception table, the moth-eaten wedding gown still worn by the elderly, left-at-the-alter bride.

Sad and horrifying all at the same time.

It sent shivers down her back. She knew that Mark's parents had died on an icy interstate in Michigan, but had it actually been on Christmas day? Since she and Mark would be spending their very first Christmas together, it was quite important that she knew whether this was the case or not. She had been living with this man for over six months now, but still didn't feel like she knew him very well. Mark was always kind—*jovial* actually, was a good word to describe him—but he was closed-up at the same time. Meggie wanted *in*. She suspected that dealing with the traumatic event of suddenly losing his parents was the key to unlocking the door to Mark's heart. She knew he was crazy about her, but there was something missing ... a *depth* to his feelings for her. Meggie was very deeply in love with Mark, and she wanted him to feel the same way about her.

He certainly *said* all the right things, but they lacked a certain degree of conviction—not in the way he said them, but in the way Meggie perceived them. They seemed to be sexually compatible, though Meggie had very limited experience in that area, and what she had experienced was wrong … filthy and perverted. She still had not confided her past to Mark. What would be the point? Besides, Meggie did not want to give Mark any reason to think badly of her, or worse yet, to ask her to leave. Mark had revealed that he had "played around" some in college, but had never had a "girlfriend" per se. Meggie wondered if Mark was even *capable* of giving his heart away. Was it because of his enormous loss? Maybe Meggie should confront Mark with his past and help counsel him through it … but no … she was coming up with a much better idea!

Present Day

Late June would quickly be giving way to summer …
glorious summer in Northern Michigan! It had been almost
six weeks since Meggie had initially asked Mark to rig up
some kind of pen for Mel, but as yet, there had been no
sign of hammer and nails. The situation with Mel was
becoming imminent and dire.

Over the past week, Ryan had inexplicably become almost
like a family member, coming and going both without
invitation or limitation. He never failed to take Meggie's
hand, raise it to his lips, gazing into her eyes and telling her
that he was "at your service". It was thrilling and
disconcerting to Meggie, but she liked it … she liked it
very much. Knowing Meggie's love for the French
language, he had taken to calling her, "Mon'Amie", which
was charming the socks off her. It was harmless, as it only
meant, "My friend", though it was said in a hushed,
clandestine tone that suggested otherwise. Mark was often
in the room, but completely oblivious to the growing
tension between Meggie and Ryan … *sexual tension*, that
is, which Meggie herself was fighting desperately to ignore.
This was difficult since Ryan had no problem invading
Meggie's personal space, and didn't try to even hide his
amorous inclinations toward her. Mark seemed to take it in
stride, like it was just another one of Ryan's jokes or
impersonations. He'd laugh. That's right—*laugh*! As
though Meggie wasn't worthy of such intentions, and that it
could only be perceived as jocular. This infuriated Meggie,

while creating more of the very insecurity that Mark was so good at bringing out in her. Maybe Mark was right. Maybe Ryan was joking around. But it certainly didn't *feel* that way to Meggie. She was 99.9 percent sure that he meant it, whatever *it* was. This flirtation was proving to be quite an inspiration to Meggie's plans for self-improvement. Whenever Ryan looked longingly into Meggie's luminescent, hazel eyes, they were now fringed with mascara-lengthened, dark lashes. She had started to curb her enthusiasm for fattening foods, and had begun a regular work-out schedule. In fact, she had decided to get back into Tae Kwon Do and join in on the Saturday morning class in which Ryan happened to be a student.

And so, this was how Meggie discovered that Mark actually *knew* that clawing Cheshire cat from the restaurant.

She thought it might be a good idea to just show up and observe the class so she could see what she would be up against. Mark had created an "observation room" with a one-way mirror for parents to be able to watch their kids without intimidating or distracting them. It also kept the parents from being able to verbalize their two-cents of advice or to criticize Mark while he taught, which parents were prone to do. Meggie entered the small room and made her way to the top of the three tiers of graduated benches. Nobody else was in the room with her. Meggie's eyes were first drawn to Mark—tall, handsome, agile, and obviously having a great deal of fun teaching this class. Her attention then found Ryan, shorter than Mark, but more muscular in a compact sort of way. His movements were quick, forceful and exacting. He appeared to be taking the work-out very seriously, and looked seriously dangerous. He was positioned at the center of the first of two rows—directly in front of Mark. There were three students on either side of him, and seven in the second row. Meggie's focus was pulled to a shimmering swish of a long, black ponytail. The tall, slender owner of this mane somehow wore her uniform in a way that suggested it was custom-fitted. OH. MY. GOD. thought Meggie, as she realized at whom she was looking.

NO ... WAY. Bile crept into the back of Meggie's throat as she observed the girl glancing repeatedly between Mark and Ryan as she tried to keep up. She was graceful and coordinated, but did not have the moves down. Normally, Mark would have new class members stay in the back so as not to distract others, but here she was, front and center, right next to Ryan. Meggie wanted to bolt, but it was as if she were glued to the seat, unable to tear away from the horror show. She watched the girl fumble the moves, giggle inappropriately, look around to inventory just how many were looking at her, toss her ponytail, then resume the routine. It was obvious that she felt entitled to being the center of attention. Mark normally did not put up with this kind of behavior! It was sickening.

The class ended, and Meggie cracked the door just enough so she could watch the students leave the studio. Mark came out first, with Ryan right behind him. Mark made it a habit to bow to each student as they left as a sign of respect. It appeared that Ryan was joining him in this effort as he stood by Mark's side. The bimbo brunette was the last to exit the studio, giving Meggie the opportunity to watch as she strategically pulled strands of her hair out of the ponytail to frame her face "just so" and adjusted her uniform to accentuate her assets. She then painted on a breathless-looking smile and literally pranced out into the vestibule to greet Mark and Ryan. Both men looked practically rapturous as she bounced up upon them. She sidled up to Ryan, who, *unbelievably*, draped his arm casually around her shoulders. Meggie was seething as she listened to the two of them gush over what a "Great job, Whitney!" had done. Whitney. Dim-Whit, more like. Oh, what a big, happy family the three of them made. Meggie debated whether or not to emerge from the observation room, but seemed to be frozen there. Meggie continued to watch and listen as Mark told Whitney how glad he was that she was in the class and how "deceptively" good she was. *Deceptively good?* Those were the same words Mark had used when he and Meggie had met at the Boston competition! How dare he?

Mark then excused himself, after which the tramp extricated herself from Ryan's almost-embrace, saying, "See ya next time!" in that phony, high-pitched, grating voice of hers. Ryan watched her go, and then turned to follow Mark into the office. Meggie took this opportunity to hightail it out of there, tears stinging her eyes and pulse pounding in her ears. She was most definitely not going to be a part of *this* class!

Later in the day, Mark and Ryan came back to the house to find Meggie in the back yard, lugging two-by-fours, hammer, nails and an old, rusty saw out to the area just beyond their patio furniture. Although it appeared that she was setting out to build something, she didn't look quite capable of the job. In fact, she looked awfully cute, in a pair of faded dungaree overalls with the legs cut off to an almost Daisy Duke degree of shortness. She had a bathing suit top underneath, which lent a flair of femininity to the ensemble. Plus, she was actually wearing make-up, just a little, but enough to highlight her best features. She had her strawberry-blonde hair pulled into a high ponytail, with gentle whisps falling over her eyes in a carefully arranged disheveled way.

"What on earth are you doing, Meg?" asked Mark as they made their way across the yard toward her. His tone would have sounded amused, had the listener not understood the manipulation taking place. Meggie turned around, absently tucked her fly-away hair behind her ear, and brightly responded with an obviously forced smile,

"Building a dog pen! What do you think?"

"Oh for God's sake ..." said Mark, turning to Ryan for some kind of support. "Meg, you are *not* building a dog pen. Just put that stuff down."

Ryan looked from Mark to Meg, then back to Mark again. He already knew about this point of contention, and didn't miss a beat,

"This woman sure knows how to light a fire under someone's lazy butt - either that, or she just married the wrong guy!" and then started to laugh as he added,

"Hey – you know, last year I joined a supp... procrastinators – but they haven't met ye...

Although neither Mark nor Meggie fo... humorous, they laughed as well. It eased... the tension remained, just under the surface, for... malcontented couple.

"Meggie, *I promise*, I'll start on it tomorrow ..."

Meggie dropped the tools that were still in her hands right there on the spot, saying, "Tomorrow. Good, then. Hey Ryan, you hungry?" but thinking to herself, *Married the wrong guy? What does he mean by that?* It made her heart leap, and joy toward Ryan replaced the anger she had felt toward Mark.

"*Je pense que je te aime,*" said Meggie over her shoulder to Ryan as he followed her like a puppy dog into the house.

"What? What was that you said?" as he pulled gently and playfully on her ponytail.

Meggie just grinned at him, but surprised herself by her brazenness.

Mark followed in a manner resembling a scolded dog with his tail between his legs. Even if he had heard what she'd said, he wouldn't have known what it meant—and wouldn't have asked.

90

probably be a much happier person if she could simply keep her expectations low—very low where Mark was concerned. She cursed him under her breath, thinking again of Ryan's strange and daring words about her "marrying the wrong guy". These words had been repeating themselves in her mind ever since Ryan had uttered them. It was like a mantra, and taking on a life of its own.

Meggie sat at her make-up table, resentfully getting ready for work. She suddenly noticed a lost eyelash resting on her cheek, and reached up to brush it away. She stopped short and thought to herself,

When did I stop wishing on eyelashes?

So instead of brushing it away, she gently wiped with her index finger and held the fateful lash balanced on the tip. She closed her eyes tightly, made a desperate wish, and forcefully blew it off.

I want a DO-OVER in my marriage!

She regarded her reflection in the illuminated table-top mirror, and thought about that for a minute.

What a dumb wish. Did I waste the eyelash?

Obviously, there would be no "do-overs", just endings, and then new beginnings.

You can't go back in time, for crying out loud.

Was it too late to re-word her wish? What exactly did Meggie want? If only Mark weren't such a jerk sometimes! There were times that Meggie truly believed that Mark didn't even love her. That he was plainly incapable of love. The loss of his parents had certainly done a number on him. What else could it be? She thought back to their first Christmas together. Her grand plan to give Mark the "therapy" she just knew would do the trick and help free him from his emotional bondage to the past ...

and imaginary, from November until April of the new year.
In both Boston and Maine, it was always mixed with slush
and dirty, salty road plow embankments—not pretty, and
definitely not magical.

Sometimes though, as a child, Meggie would awaken to the
incredible stillness of a new snowfall. The mere
peacefulness of the event would be a sound not heard, but
rather, *felt*. It was this feeling that would arouse her to
consciousness, pulling her trance-like to the window, to
watch as her world was blanketed with frozen fairy
teardrops, each flake intricate and unique. The streetlights
would cast a diffused glow, causing the ground to appear
covered in multi-faceted diamonds and jewels. With her
child's fierce imagination, she would wish that there were
real diamonds out there, just waiting for her to go out and
collect. She could sell them and then buy a big mansion on
a lake somewhere for her and her mother to live. Maybe her
mother would realize that she didn't need some stupid man,
and then she and Meggie could be happy—just the two of
them—and rich, rich *rich*!

Meggie almost smiled at this memory, but the loneliness of
the reality of it made that impossible. Those were just

moments in time ... flights of fancy that served as temporary escapes for a very troubled and sad child.

Meggie shook it off, thinking to herself how lucky she was to have met and fallen in love with someone like Mark. And here was her opportunity to help him! Meggie herself may never overcome her past, but then, she did not seem to be affected by it the way Mark was by his. She had given her entire heart, freely and eagerly to Mark. 100 percent. All she wanted was for him to return the favor—*was that too much to ask?*

It was late. Mark was asleep, soundly and warmly in their king-sized heated waterbed. Meggie loved their awesomely comfortable bed, and sharing it with Mark every night.

Earlier that day, she had carried down all the mothball-smelling packages from the attic. She had lovingly wiped the dirt and dust off as best she could, then re-taped areas that were torn. She even applied some new, brightly colored ribbons and bows to help turn the Christmas past into Christmas present.
Hey! *That's* what she'd say to Mark in the morning as the surprise was revealed ...

Here sweetie, a Christmas long past turned into Christmas "presents"!

Meggie wondered if Mark had simply forgotten about these poor, unopened gifts. Opening them, with Meggie at his side, should provide a release of that bottled up pain, and at the same time bring a sense of joy and love, which

This was going to be the most wonderful, spectacular, fantastic Christmas of Meggie's life—and hopefully Mark's!

arms and kissing her gently on the lips. The kiss quickly became more urgent, moving from lips to neck to breast. Mark breathlessly whispered back, "Merry Christmas, love ... let me give you one of your presents a little *early* ..."

A couple of hours later, they sat in armchairs by the tree, sipping their coffee laden with Bailey's Irish Cream, Kahlua, and topped with luscious whipped cream. Meggie had prepared their coffee drinks while Mark got a fire going in the fireplace. They watched the colorful flames dance and crackle, as Andy Williams crooned "Let it Snow" from the record player, as it did just that outside. At first, Mark did not even take notice of the packages, nearly bursting at the seams with their history, scattered under the sparsely decorated tree. But as the caffeine entered his bloodstream, bringing him out of his morning drowsy, post love-making state, he began to look around in appreciation of the transformed living room.

Meggie peered over the rim of her cup as she sipped, watching Mark's face as he finally did notice the pile of gifts.

She watched with growing alarm as his expression changed from good-humored amusement, to curiosity, clearly then changing to confusion, followed by shocked recognition, and finally to a smoldering mixture of fury and apparent distress. It was as if it was happening in slow motion, frame-by-frame. Meggie's own emotions fluctuated along with Mark's, which she could feel vicariously as though they were her own. That doubt and fear, that had obviously been telling her something earlier, crept back in spades as she hesitantly ventured,

"Mark? … Surprise …" she faltered in a weak voice.

"What on earth, Meggie? What have you done?" This was said with such an undeniable tinge of accusation that Meggie physically cringed, and choked on her coffee.

All of a sudden, the room felt cold, despite the warm ambience she had worked so hard to create. Andy Williams' voice took on a tinny quality as they sat there, not knowing what to say to each other.

Then Mark silently stood up, and without so much as a glance at Meggie, turned and stiffly walked toward the staircase. Meg listened to his footsteps as they ascended, and then heard the bedroom door close—not slamming exactly, but shut with a kind of finality that rocked Meggie to her core.

She didn't know what to do.

His voice and manner were restrained as he leaned over Meggie with his hands on the armrests on either side of her chair.

"Meg. I don't know how or *why* you got into my personal stuff—*my personal stuff*—but I'm going to give you the benefit of the doubt and assume your intentions were good. However, I want you to put *all* this back where it came from—*now*—and I want you to promise that you will never do anything like that again. I'm going out for a run." And then he pushed himself up and away from her with an exaggerated effort, and was out the door.

Meggie did as she was told, leaving only the recently purchased gifts to each other under the tree, which didn't get opened until New Year's Day. So, this was their first Christmas together. And they would not speak of it again until years later ... when it was almost too late.

It was proving too much for her to hold in.

She and Mark were sitting at the kitchen table, eating some stir-fry as a light and easy supper. To spice up the meal a bit, they were drinking Hot Sake, which had been warmed up in the microwave. Meggie had already quaffed two rather large cups of the potent liquid as she had fried up the rice and vegetables. It had loosened her tongue, and you know what they say about loose lips …

"Mark." She began, saying his name in a way that a school teacher might call out a misbehaving student.

He looked up and replied, mimicking her tone.

"What?"

"Why did you pretend not to know Whitney when we were at *Amical*?"

"What are you talking about, Meg?"

"What do you mean, what am I talking about? You know what I'm talking about! And you know that … that … *La Chienne*!"

"La what?"

"*La Chienne. La Putain. La Pouffiasse.*" These were scandalous names Meggie had memorized just in order to describe Whitney.

"Come on, Meg. Just say what it is you want to say."

"Mark! Why won't you respond appropriately? You *know* her! Whitney? The restaurant? Your class on Saturday morning? Come on … *McFly* … *anyone home*?" She reached over to knock on Mark's forehead to emphasize his stupidity.

"Knock it off, *Biff* … and Meggie—I *don't* know her," as he reached up to grab her hand angrily away. "At least I didn't when we were at the restaurant. And yes, she is now a student. *So what*?"

"Why didn't you *tell* me?"

"I don't tell you every time I get a new student!"

"But *her*? You should have told me! You should have told her that the class was full! You should have *known* how it would make me feel! I HATE that girl!"

"Meggie—you have got to get past your insecurity. It is not an attractive personality trait. It's pretty pitiful, really. You should hear yourself."

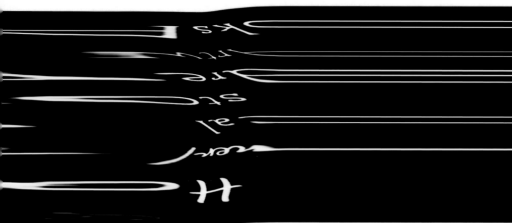

bath on the *roof?* Right Mark. And she could have said NO to King David when he summoned her for a little romp in the hay!"

"That's just it, Meg—who says no to a king?"

"Unbelievable, Mark. This is such a stupid conversation. And if you're going to compare her to a figure in the Bible—I think that Jezebel or Delilah might be better choices!"

"Meggie—get a handle on your jealousy."

"Can't you see, Mark? I'm not jealous of her, or anyone for that matter. I just hate the way you act whenever you see a pretty woman. It's *you*—not me! You're *killing* me! And you're killing US!"

And with that, she fled out of the room, toppling her plate to the floor with a clatter. She ran up the stairs and slammed the bedroom door with enough force to create a shudder in the walls of the old farmhouse.

Mark did not follow her. She waited, sitting alert and agitated on the bed—staring at the door in such a way as to *will* it to open and reveal Mark standing there, penitent and understanding. It remained closed. Mark slept on the couch that night.

Meggie hardly slept a wink. She so desperately wanted to tiptoe down the stairs, put her arms around her husband and ask him to come up to their bed. But that might require an apology on her part. And what exactly should she be sorry for? As devastated as she was over their fight, she was also frustrated by the way Mark would *always* manage to turn it around and make it *her* problem. How could she verbalize the way Mark's flirtations made her feel without sounding like a jealous fool? In their nine years of marriage, they had not spoken to each other with the harshness and coldness of the evening's unfinished battle. And unfinished it would remain, as for Meggie, there was no way to win. The feeling of defeat that came with this knowledge served no purpose other than to pull her self-esteem further into oblivion. She truly wondered what was wrong with her. She finally fell asleep, but with her heart pounding painfully in her chest—empty and abandoned. *Mark doesn't love me* ... was her final thought as her awareness became restless slumber.

Meggie awoke the next morning to the muffled sounds of hammering and an electric saw buzzing away in the back yard. Her heart leapt as she opened her eyes and realized that Mark was *finally* building the dog pen! She took this to mean that he was trying to make up somehow for last night's argument, and that it was his way of showing her just how important she really was to him! She jumped out of bed, grabbed her bathrobe, and almost flew down the stairs.

When she saw Mark still sprawled over the couch, snoring in a deep sleep, she stopped in her tracks. Had she only imagined the sounds of carpentry?

Meg made her way into the kitchen and peered out the window over the sink. No, she had not imagined it. There was Ryan, in a pair of faded and frayed blue-jeans, perfectly fitted over his sculpted back-side. He was also wearing a Woodstock t-shirt, and a baseball cap turned backwards. His Buddy Holly glasses were obviously, "transitions", and had transformed into sunglasses in the bright morning light. Amazingly, the pen he was in the process of building was already perfectly framed out. He definitely knew what he was doing, and he looked good doing it.

About this time, Mark shuffled into the kitchen, joining Meggie at the window.

"What's going on?" His morning breath as much an affront as his laziness.

Meg turned to glare at him. "Apparently, your *friend* is building a dog pen in our backyard."

"*What?*" Mark cracked the back door and looked out in disbelief. "Oh man ... Hey, Meg—would you please make some coffee for us?" as he pushed the door open to join

help you out and get started on it. God knows you've sure helped me with my Tae Kwon Do … just returning the favor, buddy!"

Mark was dumbfounded. Meggie could easily read the emotions on his face. It was a mixture of embarrassment, annoyance, gratitude, and relief. He quickly made the choice to go with the latter and responded a little too enthusiastically, an octave or two higher than his usual vocal range,

"Well, *thanks*, man—this was sure unexpected … and unnecessary. But you shouldn't be doing this by yourself. Let me get changed and we'll work on it together. Meg's making coffee … want some?"

****

The dog pen was ready by the end of the day – sturdy and well built – and not a minute too soon. Mel's litter came into the world the very next day. It was as if the animal knew somehow that this was her space; she had eagerly been led into it once it was finished, and had slept there that night. Meggie had gone to the Tractor Supply store to purchase a bale of hay to spread in the pen as bedding, and then put out a couple of pans for both food and water. Mel gave birth to her "fatherless" pups in what Meg could only compare to as a "manger".

But *oh*! The puppies were adorable! Slipping and sliding all over each other with their tiny tails wagging happily as they greedily latched onto their mother's teats—their one and only concern in their newborn life. Ryan showed up a couple of hours after the final pup was born to find Meggie inside the pen, her back against the wooden slats, knees drawn up to her chest … and bawling. He climbed in and sat next to her, putting his arm around her. She turned her face into his massive warm shoulder and saturated his t-shirt with her tears. Neither spoke, until Meggie finally pulled away, wiped at her wet cheeks and eyes, and huskily croaked out, "I'm sorry," and climbed out of the pen. She slowly trudged across the grass to the house, and disappeared through the back door. Ryan watched her through his somewhat foggy lenses, reaching up to gingerly caress the tear-soaked shirt sleeve. He understood wholly the source of those tears, and was secretly glad for them. The next thing he knew, he heard the snapping of sneakered soles slapping up the driveway, followed by the

athlete. "Just born this morning then?" he asked, though the
answer was obvious.

"Yeah. Meggie couldn't stop crying. There was no
consoling her. I don't know if she was just overwhelmed by
the miracle of birth, or what."

"D,ya think she could have been crying for any other
reason?"

"What? Like maybe she wants a baby of her own or
something?"

Ryan considered this for a minute. "I hadn't actually
thought of that ... but *does* she?"

Mark was silent for a minute, and then turned to walk away
as he muttered, "I don't know ... I just don't know
anything anymore," leaving Ryan to mull it all over alone
in the hay.

****

Ryan made a living in the insurance industry. He had been a salesman, but now specialized in claims – mostly automobile. His "home office" was the second of the two-bedroom apartment he was living in. He did most of his work from here, and felt pretty lucky to be able to schedule his own hours, and work all day in his underwear if he so chose. He did have to go out to inspect damage when claims were made, but he was able to schedule those at his own convenience as well. At one point, he had attempted to use his position and expertise to spend some one-on-one with Meggie, telling both Mark and Meggie that he could likely save them some money on their auto policies if they'd make a switch to his company. He knew that Meggie was the one who made those kinds of decisions in their household, as well as being the one who paid the bills, and that Mark would have had no interest. He had thought for sure that she would have been interested in saving some money and would meet with him to discuss it, but so far, they had not taken him up on it.

He was absently flipping through some recent memos and updates, as his mind kept drifting to thoughts of Meggie. He couldn't seem to stop thinking about her! She was everything he had always hoped for in a woman – beautiful, while being totally unaware of her beauty, intelligent, hard-working, a pretty decent cook ... and he loved the way she had decorated their farmhouse. The very first time he had walked into Mark and Meggie's house, he had felt a loving warmth emanating from the atmosphere she had created. He remembered the pride just oozing from

quite a selfish side of himself on several occasions. And he could really be flirtatious, and *not* with his wife! In fact, Mark seemed to flirt *more* when Meggie was around to watch. Ryan could tell that it hurt her. It made him wonder if Mark was actually trying to hurt Meg. Ryan was starting to wonder, hopefully, if the two of them weren't even happy in their marriage.

It suddenly occurred to Ryan just how he could manage to spend some one-on-one with Meggie. He'd start looking for a house!

Ryan decided to mention it to Mark first, hoping that Mark would actually make the *suggestion* that Ryan use Meggie as his agent. But when the subject of his house-hunting came up following class on Saturday, Mark had seemed uncomfortable. In fact, it was appearing to Ryan that Mark was beginning to distance himself. It was kind of weird, and had the effect of making Ryan feel a little guilty. He hadn't even done anything – yet! Could Mark be sensing that Ryan's motives toward Meggie were a threat? As far as Ryan was concerned, Mark only had himself to blame. The stupid guy had a precious gem, but spent no time polishing it. Meggie deserved better. Meggie deserved a guy like

Ryan. But if his relationship with Mark went south he would lose access to Meg.

He needed to throw Mark off the trail somehow, and knew just how to do it. He quickly changed the subject, asking Mark if he and Meggie might like to go on a double-date that evening.

"Really man!? So who are you dating?" he asked with sudden great interest.

"It's a surprise!" Ryan said with a smile and a wink. Hopefully Whitney would say yes, he thought to himself.

****

Her scent preceded her. That same sexy-spicy scent … what was it? Patchouli? With a hint of some spice … clove, maybe? Meggie knew who Ryan's date was before she had even become physically visible. Her face turned three shades of red, bordering on purple as anger, dread and insecurity took its hold upon her.

"Hey!" came that voice, a decibel or two louder than was necessary. Mark stood up, gentleman that he was, and allowed the hussy to kiss his cheek as Meggie watched, desperately trying to compose herself. Mark's eyes, widely innocent, locked onto Meggie's as he mouthed the words, *I didn't know*!

Ryan echoed Whitney's greeting, "Hey!" and sat down in the empty chair next to Meg, casually draping his arm across the back of her chair.

"Well, Ryan," said Meg in a tone that did not hide her jealousy or discomfort very well, "do I not get a peck on the cheek from *you*?" The minute she said it she realized how ridiculous it sounded. But Ryan didn't flinch. His kiss was more intimate than just a peck on the cheek, as it landed on her ear, with just the slightest suggestion of a nibble – or was it her imagination? Nobody else at the table seemed to notice anything unusual about it, and Ryan eased back into his own space as cool as a refrigerated cucumber. He quickly introduced Whitney to Meggie, but left no room for the usual niceties when introductions were made, and instead went right into entertainment mode, telling a joke

smiled weakly and insincerely at each other, neither
mentioning their initial encounter at *Amical*. Meggie's
stomach was in knots.

"Soooo ... this is nice." Ryan said, still in entertainer mode,
impersonating Timon from *Lion King*. Then, "We've never
had the chance to double-date before."

"You never told us you were dating anyone," responded
Meg quickly.

"Well, this is just the first of hopefully many to come ..."
Ryan's glance went from Whitney to Mark, as if to
evaluate each of their reactions.

Mark mirrored Ryan's movements, and looking from Ryan
to Whitney, and then back to Ryan, he said,

"The big question is, what on earth does she see in a guy
like you?"

But the minute it came out of his mouth, Meggie could see
that look of regret overcome his face. She knew it well.
Whenever he stuck his huge, stinky foot into his mouth he
seemed to simultaneously realize the asininity of his words.
Most of the time he was too pig-headed or embarrassed to

retract them. Meggie found it very hard to comprehend why Mark never seemed capable of *thinking* before speaking. She was also aware and astute in her careful observations of Ryan's sense of insult with these words – though he hid it well.

He went into *Austin Powers* mode, placing his pinky to the side of his chin with the hand out-turned, and addressing Whitney said in perfect character, "Oh baby – just *tell* them. Tell them that you just want to *shag* me baby!"

Whitney came back with a quick reply, mimicking Ryan with her own version of *Austin Powers*, saying, "Oh be*have*!"

Mark laughed as though this was the most hilarious thing he'd heard in years. "See Meggie?" He managed in-between his ridiculous, phony guffaws, "They're a match made in heaven!"

Meggie was not pleased, nor was she amused, but she gave a quick smile that bordered on a snarl, and slurped down the rest of her Mojito.

This prompted Mark to notice that their companions did not have drinks yet. He signaled to the waitress, a very cute girl to whom Mark had already commented on her amazing resemblance to the beautiful Ann-Margaret, *when she was young, that is*. The waitress had no idea to whom Mark was referring, so he went on to explain that Ann-Margaret had been a sex-symbol in her day – a true knock-out beauty …

Meggie just cringed as she waited for Mark to stop gushing. She had to give this waitress credit though; she handled the unsolicited flirtation with a professional, cool-

Can I get you two something to drink besides water?

Ryan looked towards Mark's glass, filled with creamy-looking dark ale.

"What's that you're drinking?"

"Dragon's Milk. If you've never had it I would highly recommend it – best dark beer on the planet – smooth, rich, with a hint of chocolate and toasted vanilla. Even Meggie likes it, and she doesn't like beer!"

"Sounds good. I'll take what he's drinking then."

"Ditto," said Whitney.

Meggie stared at her own glass, *willing* Mark to notice that she was on empty and suggest a refill (much in the way she held out hope that he might notice when her car's gas tank was running low and then take it upon himself to fill it for her). But it was the waitress who noticed.

"Can I get you another Mojito?"

"You know ... I think I'll have a Dragon's Milk instead."

"Meggie! You know those kick butt! Are you sure?"

Meggie glared at Mark for a second or two, and then rested her gaze upon the pretty and kind waitress. "A Dragon's Milk, please."

"Coming right up!" and as she turned from the table, she and Meggie exchanged an understanding kind of look. Her tip just went up by 5% thought Meggie.

Poppycock's was another one of Meggie's favorite restaurants in Traverse City. Luckily, they made the absolute *best* burger in town, which made it easy to talk Mark into going there. He always ordered the burger. So as the four of them perused the menu, Mark expounded on the irresistible attributes of *Poppycock's* burger. This made Ryan's choice easy. Meg decided upon the Butternut Squash Ravioli in browned-butter-walnut and sage sauce. Whitney's choice was a Caesar salad, but light on the dressing and no shaved parmesan or croutons thank-you-very-much.

Really? thought Meggie as she visualized the girl's perfect, fat-free figure. Was it worth the sacrifice of great-tasting food for the sake of beauty? Well, right now she was *really* hungry, so the answer was a resounding *no*.

The waitress returned with their drinks, and some soft, hot rolls with seasoned dipping oil. She took their dinner orders and slipped away.

The awkward stage began.

"So, Whitney ... what do you do?" inquired Mark.

"I thought you already knew. I work with Ryan – selling

"That's okay! It's not really worth remembering. Sometimes I even forget what I do!" Whitney returned with a silly giggle.

"Meggie," explained Ryan, "Whitney is also taking Mark's Saturday morning Tae Kwon Do class." Though as Ryan was saying it, Meggie could tell that he knew that she was already aware of this fact, but she didn't say anything to reveal that she knew that he knew that she knew.

Had Mark told Ryan about Meggie's so-called "jealousy"? And if so, it would be pretty cruel of Ryan to bring this girl on a double-date with them, wouldn't it?

Meggie was feeling some pretty confusing and upsetting emotions.

"So how do you like selling insurance?" continued Mark, ignoring Ryan's comment to Meggie, and obviously trying to change *that* subject.

"Ummm ... I don't know. It's a job. Mostly I sell car insurance, so it's pretty easy, I mean, everyone who drives has to have it. A necessary evil, I guess. Most people don't understand the lingo or the fine print, which can be a pain

"You mean, Whitney and *I* ..." interrupted Meg, immediately turning red when she realized that it was Ryan, *not* Mark whose grammar she was correcting.

"Hmmm ... let's go back to that bit about most people not understanding the fine print. Say someone is out driving in the winter, and suddenly drives into a white-out, and didn't see or know that another car had stopped right in front of them, hidden by the white-out, therefore hitting that car. Would you go to bat for your customer so that the damage was covered, with no deductible due, and no increases on their premiums, seeing how it was unavoidable?" asked Mark.

This hypothetical-sounding example had actually happened to Meggie a couple of years before, and both Mark and Meggie had been furious about having to pay their deductible, which was quite high to keep their insane premium as low as possible.

"Well ... it doesn't work like that. First of all, this is a no-fault state –"

"Oh, don't get me started on that! It is ludicrous that people are not held accountable for their own lousy driving! I will never understand why all of us, even the best drivers, are punished for the inept and the reckless with unbelievably higher rates than the states that don't have that stupid law. Instead, they add "uninsured motorists" which is much more cost-effective and places the burden on the true driver at fault."

Ryan didn't have a good answer for that one, so instead went on to make his point, "Second of all, a white-out can almost be predicted, depending on the weather forecast, making such an accident not *sudden and accidental* which is the terminology used to explain that, and actually avoidable."

"*Avoidable*? Are you kidding? A white-out, like an earthquake or tornado, is an act of God, and *not* predictable, and certainly not avoidable!"

"There are no such things as acts of God." answered Ryan with smug, matter-of-factness.

Uh-oh, thought Meggie. This was the equivalent of striking Mark below the belt. *Them's fightin' words*. And she was right. Mark's face was slowly turning purple – the color rising from his neck as though someone had popped the top of his head open, and was pouring a deep red burgundy into it.

Whitney tried to divert Mark's attention from Ryan, defending him at the same time. "Well I don't believe in God, anyway. That kind of belief just doesn't make sense."

Meggie was exultant to hear Whitney utter these preposterous words, knowing that she would now and forever be held in Mark's deepest contempt. *There!* That shows what she's made of! All at once Meggie's concerns about Mark's impressions of this floozy just floated away. She was also pretty sure that her comment would plummet her in Ryan's esteem, but he surprised her,

"I'm not so sure I believe either. I mean, I'd like to believe – or rather, I'd like to *know*, but there's just no proof."

"That's why it's called faith, and that's why God gave us the Bible," returned Mark with measured control.

"Men wrote the Bible – not God."

"Men who were inspired by God. Men who witnessed Jesus' crucifixion and resurrection …"

"That's just a story. And it's unclear who even wrote the Gospels, so you can't say with any authority whatsoever, or any proof, that the writers witnessed *anything*."

The conversation at the table was turning from awkward to heated, and alcohol, in the form of the very potent Dragon's Milk, and on empty stomachs, was stoking the flames. Funny how appropriate the name of the delicious beer was.

Mark was really struggling to maintain his cool, but Meggie knew full well that this was striking at the very core of his *very* necessary belief system. She probably should have tried to change the subject, but this was one of her favorite topics of discussion.

Mark tried to be casually flippant, "Well ... to each his

placed in front of them. The enjoyment of their meals was then only punctuated by comments on how *excellent* the food was. When the waitress stopped by to check on how things were going, Ryan ordered another round of Dragon's Milk for the table – on him.

Uh-oh, thought Meggie again. *This ain't over.*

They were finishing up their meals when the next round arrived. Despite the veiled underpinning of mistrust, envy, frustration and even anger each felt simmering below the surface, the party had turned to one that appeared to be camaraderie to the casual observer. Meggie knew better, and knowing the volatile potential of having a faith-based debate with Mark, she was opting to keep her mouth shut. But Whitney was not going to let it go.

"So Meg. Do *you* believe in God?"

Meggie had the wherewithal to keep her answer short.

"Yes. I do."

Mark looked at her with arrogant skepticism and said, "Yeah ... *right.*"

being written by men had always bugged Meggie. And it was also just a group of men who had picked and chosen what would even be included in the Bible. How could someone *pick and choose* what was supposedly God's word? Mark's comment, and the snideness of it, was impossible for Meg to ignore.

"Mark. You *know* that I believe in God. Absolutely. Unequivocally. I believe in God even though I've never seen Him, heard Him, felt Him … I don't know what people could possibly mean when they claim to have a *personal relationship* with God. Or frankly, that they *love* God! To have a personal relationship with, or to love someone, you have to be able to hang your hat on *something*! With God as an intangible idea, I think the best we can hope for is to just believe in him. And even that's a stretch for most people. Especially when you look at the world around us! It is arrogant, arrogant, *arrogant* to act like there's something wrong with someone who has a hard time with this concept of God. And I think that the people who claim a relationship, or feelings of love toward Him, are *not* doing those who struggle one ounce of a favor or a kindness. It only makes those who are struggling with doubt feel even more inadequate, like there must be something wrong with them! I mean, how is that even possible? To have a relationship or feelings toward something you can't see, hear or feel? That's what pisses me off! *Despite all that, I still believe!* I pray for Him to fill my heart. He has yet to answer. What? Am I not worthy?"

Meggie wasn't taking a breath. Her passion on the subject was obvious, and had everyone's rapt attention.

"But the Bible?" she continued, "The jury's still out on that one. Too much of it doesn't make any sense. I guess I just think it's a book written by men who desperately wanted to understand where they came from, why they're here, and where they go when they die. But I also think that it was written during times that people needed to be controlled. This was the way of 'laying down the law' before the Constitution was written. And it was done by creating fear in many instances, and then creating hope in others. That is one of the reasons for the huge differences in the nature of God himself between the Old Testament and the New."

She took a deep breath. Her faced was deeply flushed. Anyone listening had no doubt that much thought had gone into her opinions. Her outburst had somehow defused Mark, who had only moments before been poised to ignite. He looked amusedly at Ryan and Whitney, saying,

"See what I live with? Meg and I talk about this sort of thing quite a bit actually. She makes good points, but just really doesn't understand."

And that's how it al...

Meggie; she s...

plausibl...

question...

utterly ho...

to go. Not ...

assurance as ...

was that she di...

persuasive expla...

from this world co...

Whitney pushed further.

"So how can you believe in God, something you can't see, hear or touch, but *not* believe in the Bible, which you *can* see, hear and touch?"

"Like I said, I think the Bible is man's way of answering fundamental questions that we're not really meant to understand. I believe in the tangibility of the Bible as a book, but not in the intangibility of it being God's Word. At least I haven't been convinced of it yet. As far as believing in God? To me, a supreme Creator is the *only* thing that makes sense. What I don't understand is God's nature. Not because of the contradictions between the angry, vengeful God of the Old Testament, and the forgiving, loving God of the New Testament. It's because of this *world*. It's because of the *suffering*. I just can't understand why God allows it. I just don't know what He's thinking."

"That doesn't explain *why* you believe," probed Whitney.

Both Mark and Ryan seemed to be completely entertained by the verbal interchange between the two young women, who, at first, had an impenetrable wall of stone set up between them – neither slightly interested in breaking it down.

"I don't know, Whitney. I just do. I mean, look at the beauty and power of nature, and the way life and death occurs with such precision and dependability. In many ways, human life and death reflects nature – the seasons are one example. That, in and of itself, makes me believe in reincarnation. But think about *life*! What a miracle! And not just the way our bodies work – our hearts and lungs pumping blood, nutrients and oxygen through our miles of veins to feed every cell — the delicate chemical balance our systems *must* maintain just to function. To keep us *alive*! But what about our minds? Our thoughts and feelings? Those nebulous things that make us human? Do you honestly think that it all could be a great big fluke?"

"Yeah, actually … I guess I do," said Whitney, but without a lot of conviction.

"Creation," said Mark. "It's all right there in the Bible."

"Okay, so on day one God said, 'Let there be light,' but it wasn't until day four that he supposedly created the sun, moon and stars? How could there have been light without them? Doesn't make sense …"

Meggie was impressed. She hadn't realized that Ryan had ever even read the Bible. They had never had a conversation with him like this before. She waited for Mark's explanation.

"What you obviously don't understand is that by 'light,' God meant, let there be *understanding*."

"Ohhh … so that's what He meant … so then if God wanted us to have understanding, why was the Tree of Knowledge off-limits?"

"The Tree of Knowledge was a test." Mark was so very sure.

"I've always had difficulty with this one," said Meggie, "so God creates Adam and Eve, right? And they are *totally* innocent – like babies – absolutely no knowledge of good or evil, right or wrong. They can't even comprehend what evil might be! And then God puts the Tree in the garden and tells them not to eat the fruit. And *then* God allows for the serpent to enter the garden, who talks Eve into eating the fruit. In her innocence she has no idea that what he was asking her was wrong, or disobedient, because she has *no concept* of disobedience. She trusts the serpent, just as she trusts God. So she takes a bite, and then … God's *punishment*? Pretty harsh for this so-called crime, I think."

"God didn't *allow* the serpent!"

"What do you mean? It was *Eden*! God's own creation of paradise of which he had total control!"

"It's not that simple, Meg. Adam and Eve had freedom of choice, so God didn't have *total* control."

"So, He gave them freedom of choice but forbid them the knowledge to make informed choices?"

"I told you, it's not that simple. You just don't understand."

"No, of course not. But does He have control, or not? Even if we have freedom of choice – does He intervene if necessary? Is He truly omnipotent, omniscient, and omnipresent? If we're gonna give Him credit for the good things in our lives, do we hold Him responsible for the horrible things that happen in our lives as well? If the answer is no, then why would we pray to ask Him to intervene, or to thank him for our blessings? If He's a *laissez-faire* kind of God, then what's the point in prayer?"

"The point of prayer is to show gratitude … it is meant to humble us as a reminder that there is a supreme being."

"So according to *you*, praying for something, praying for help, just doesn't work? The only reason for prayer is to give *thanks*?"

At this point, Ryan decided to throw in some comedic relief, not giving Mark the opportunity to respond to Meggie.

"So," he said, "did you hear the one about the guy who lost his job – been unemployed for months with a family of four to feed? He finally gets a call back for this great-paying job of his dreams, right? So on the morning of his interview, it's pouring down rain. He gets downtown, and for the life of him, he can't find one frigging parking spot. He's beginning to panic, cause he's gonna be late if he can't find one. So he starts praying to God. *Please, please God – find me a parking place – I swear, if you do I'll stop drinking, I'll stop gambling, I'll go to church every Sunday and even tithe ten percent of anything I make!* Right away, a spot opens up miraculously right in front of the building where his interview is. As he pulls into the space he says to God, *Oh, hey God – don't worry about it. I just found one myself!"*

The joke worked temporarily to ease the tension, but Meggie wanted Mark to explain the point of prayer, and for some reason wanted witnesses to his explanation.

"Why can't you answer my question? Either He leaves us completely to our own devices, or He blesses and smites to his own discretion. You can't have it both ways, so which is it?"

"Exactly," agreed Whitney. "How can we believe in a God who has control, when this world is so out of control?"

"God has a plan. We just don't know what it is." Mark confidently commented.

"That's what Mark believes, but I think there is *no plan*. No control whatsoever. It's up to us. I do think that God loves us, and that when we cry, He cries harder. And when we smile, He is busting at the seams with happiness."

"I like that idea," said Whitney, "but I just don't buy it."

"You don't have to Whitney," replied Meg. "But in my book, God would be ashamed of that."

There went the wall again.

Whitney didn't quite know how to respond, but said with a bit of defiance in her tone, "Well, it's a good thing that I *don't* believe in a God who would be ashamed of me then. Ryan, let's go – I'm tired."

Meggie felt oddly energized. Somehow she sensed that she had "won" some invisible war. Was it the Dragon's Milk talking? Who knew? She was ready to go too. She needed to check on the puppies. They were growing exponentially and to the point that they might possibly climb out of the pen. The time was getting close that she'd have to try to find homes for them …

They paid their respective bills and made their way to the door, Meggie and Ryan the last to walk through it. Ryan tugged on Meggie's arm before they crossed the threshold, and quietly spoke in her ear. "I really like all your thoughts Meggie – don't pay attention to Whitney, she's not the brightest bulb in the pack."

Meggie turned to regard him wordlessly as they joined Mark and Whitney. On the one hand she was thrilled to hear him say that, giving her a feeling of self-righteous superiority over Whitney, but on the other hand she felt confusion … even a small amount of pity for Whitney. If he felt that way about her, then why was he dating her?"

As they emerged from the restaurant, Ryan slid his arm around Whitney's waist and kissed her neck, further confusing Meggie. Mark reached for Meggie's hand, but for reasons she couldn't explain she pushed it away and stuck her hands safely in her pockets.

****

Finding homes for the puppies was heartbreaking business. Meggie had not expected to get *so* attached so quickly, but being well aware of the amount of work required with dog ownership, especially training a puppy, she had no desire to keep them.

She set up shop in front of Walmart with a portable lawn chair for her to sit in, and a large box for the pups, which may not have been large enough. They were already attempting to escape, climbing up all over each other. Meggie had to really keep her eye on the one they had taken to calling Houdini. He was the largest and most rotund of the litter – the one who was always the first at the "milking station" and the last to break away. Such a cute little piggy! Somehow he had figured out how to liberate himself, and had been found wandering around the yard, on the lam, exploring what freedom was like. It was at that point that Mark and Meggie realized it was time. Of course, it had ended up being Meggie's responsibility. So here she was on a beautiful early autumn morning, all set up like some kind of pan-handler at the entrance/exit to Walmart. She was unavoidable, as were the pups. And that was the plan, *and* for their cuteness to make them irresistible. Meg's original intent had been to be like some case-worker at an orphanage – grilling potential "parents" to assess their suitability and worthiness for taking one of these babies home with them. But after a couple of hours of just about every passerby picking up and cuddling the pups, saying how much they'd *love* to take one … *but* … and then plunking them back down into the box, her attitude was becoming one of desperation. Who would've thought it would be so hard to find a home for a sweet, adorable little puppy? At the end of that couple of hours, Meggie began to lie – almost.

"Oh yes, *practically* full-blooded Golden Retriever … no, sorry, no papers though – which is the only reason they're *free*! Oh … the only reason they're this dark is because they're babies. They get lighter as they get older!"

Finally. After another three hours of practically begging, the only one left was little fatso Houdini. Meggie was debating whether or not she should just take him on home and keep him, when who should pull up to the curb?

Ryan.

Meggie was tired, sweaty, and irritable, but her heart sped up as he smiled broadly at her, and she observed his muscular, tanned arm that was hanging out the window as he pointed at Houdini. "So … he's all you got left?"

She bent down to pick up the roly-poly little fellow. "Nobody wanted him," she said as she nuzzled the pup's tiny face and he simultaneously started licking her to death, tail practically whirring with his joy at such attention.

"That's not true, Meg. I want him."

Meg looked up, surprised.

"Really?" she asked hopefully. "But I thought you lived in an apartment?"

"Well that's the thing. I'm actually looking for a house to buy. Ready to put some roots down, I guess." He waited for her to volunteer her services as a Real Estate agent, but instead got,

"Wow. Seriously? Then you really *could* take Houdini!"

"Yeah …" he said, "but not until I find a place."

"Have you been pre-approved for a loan?"

"Yup."

"Well … maybe I could help?"

"Maybe you could." He smiled with great satisfaction.

Later that evening, Meggie felt both exhilarated and terrified. Was Ryan her newest client? That could mean spending hours together – alone -- touring available homes, traversing Traverse City … What would Mark think about *that*?

Meggie wasn't sure what she had expected when she told Mark about it as he finally joined her in their bedroom after watching TV all night as she read in bed.

"Oh yeah," he said with mild interest. "He mentioned something about wanting to get a house. Do you think he's considering marrying Whitney?"

This thought had not even occurred to Meg, and for reasons she couldn't justify, it felt as though she had been slapped in the face. Could that be why he was looking for a house? Is that what he'd meant about putting down roots? Mark sure knew and spent more time with Ryan than Meggie did, which she only did along with Mark. What on earth could she have been thinking anyway? Meggie had just been hoping … *Mon Dieu* … hoping *what*? Was she making more of this than it was? Why did she even want it to be more than it obviously was? Meggie couldn't help it, but this thought was making her feel betrayed by Ryan. And it hurt. How ridiculous was that? But she rolled toward Mark and brightly said, "Maybe!" then rolled back over before her expression betrayed her innermost thoughts and feelings.

****

On her way into the office the next morning, Meg had sternly reprimanded herself for her absurdity, and vowed that she would not allow Ryan's suggestive flirtations to get the best of her. After all, she was a professional. As she sat at her desk, scanning her computer screen for any new listing on TAAR's agent's site, a cold sweat would come over her every time she heard the telephone ring. The receptionist routed the calls, one-by-one, to the appropriate recipient, none of which were Meggie. It was hard to concentrate. She was lost in her scattered thoughts when a tap-tap-tap on her door frame was followed by,

"Groovy office, baby!" in his Austin Powers alter-ego.

Meggie pretended to be annoyed, as if she were in the middle of a very important time-crunched project, and that Ryan was an intrusion, but the desperate look of relief at the sight of him was one she couldn't hide. He recognized this, and in his customary Ryan-fashion, walked around her desk, reached down to pick her hand up from it, drew it to his lips and whispered, "At your service ..." She was intensely aware of how his warm, soft, moist lips felt against her skin. Something deep within her groin area involuntarily went *twang*.

Ryan quickly moved back to the front of her desk, clapped his hands together and rubbed them back and forth briskly in an *'okay-what's-the-game-plan'* kind of way, asking Meggie,

"So … wanna help me buy a house?"

She laughed and looked down at her desk self-consciously.

"Sure! I'm not one to look a gift-horse commission in the mouth!"

"And a commission you will get! I would not make a home purchase without your expert guidance, Miss Meg."

So for the next hour or so, they went over the criteria. Meg was shocked at Ryan's "price ceiling," not realizing how much money he made … or *had*. Apparently he was doing quite well for himself. As they discussed what he was looking for in a house, his description was practically identical to the house of Meggie's dreams. She tried to recollect if any of that had ever come up in conversation with Ryan. She *did* tend to talk about it a good bit. It was truly uncanny how he was, down to the details, looking for a home that Meggie would just die for. And Ryan could afford it! Meggie didn't ask him for any of his pre-approval paperwork, which she normally required before working with a buyer. She already had a good idea of which listings she wanted to show him. She printed them up for him to look over, and get back to her once he had narrowed it down.

"I'd like to see all of them," he said.

"But you haven't looked them over yet!"

"All of them," he repeated.

She laughed a little nervously, and replied, "I'll have to set them up … can you give me a day to work it all out?"

"I'll give you all the time you need."

These words stirred something in the recesses of her memory – it gave her a wistful feeling for a moment, but she brushed it off. Trying to be professional, she stood up and offered her hand to shake Ryan's. He extended his own, and at the end of their handshake didn't quite let go, allowing for a pulling sensation as his hand and fingers gently slid away.

"Wonderful. I'll look forward to your call." and was gone as quickly as he had arrived.

Meggie was so excited she could hardly stand it, and simultaneously couldn't stand that she was excited.

****

Ominous anticipation and apprehension filled Meggie's sleep. Something huge and life-changing was about to happen. She knew it, but didn't *want* to know it. She was ecstatically happy, but devastatingly sad. Irrationally hopeful, yet paralyzingly petrified. She felt selfishly deserving, but overwhelmingly guilty. She was justifiably angry, and at the same time shamefully sorry. Her anger was toward Mark. He was practically throwing her at Ryan. How could he be so *obtuse*? Meggie was quite certain that Ryan had absolutely no intention of marrying Whitney. Could Mark really believe that? Could he be so blind as not to see what was happening between Ryan and Meggie right in front of his face? Why wasn't he protecting his turf? *Doesn't he care?* This was what was keeping Meggie torturously tossing and turning all night.

The next morning brought rain, lightning and thunder. The kind of morning that made Meggie want to linger in bed, spooning with Mark, listening to the storm, and watching the lightning flash at the window. But Mark had already swung his legs over the side of the bed and was stretching as he pushed the covers from his lap. Meggie reached up her hand and placed it gently against his back.

"Mark?" she questioned.

"Yeah?" not turning around.

"We really need to talk." she ventured.

"About what?" still facing away from her.

"Our marriage needs help, Mark. We need counseling." as she began to cry.

His back stiffened as if to throw her hand off. He stood to hover over her without an ounce of compassion, or seeming to have any interest in discussing this very important matter.

"*You* need counseling, Meggie – *not me*. And if you think you need to – then go! *Just go!*" and with that he left her with the rain beating heavily on the tin roof of their little farmhouse.

A switch was flipped within Meggie's heart. Mark's words had somehow reached into her like some big bony, jabby finger and just popped that toggle as she pleaded with him to fix their marriage. It had the effect of turning all those emotions off in Meggie that would have prevented her from surrendering to Ryan. She was filled with only those cold and turbulent thoughts that somehow made her want to get some kind of revenge for Mark's callousness. But what good was revenge when he didn't give a flying flip in the first place? Even so, the pain of it was almost unbearable. He had most definitely answered her question of whether he cared or not. It was *not* the answer she had desperately hoped for, and had crucially needed.

A little later that same morning, Meggie sat by herself on the back porch, contemplating the small black spider who so bravely and defiantly kept respinning the web she had swiped down umpteen times. This morning Meggie had come outside and almost fiercely swept it down in frustration. But now ... now she was coming to the realization in that "keeping house" she was inadvertently destroying the house of the tiny spider. It hadn't mattered how many times she had obliterated the web in the corner. The arachnid would diligently just create another during the night – and in the same location. What was the definition of insanity? Doing the same thing, over and over, expecting a different result. So maybe the spider was insane. Meggie could relate. She was just like that spider, spinning and spinning, trying to create a home. Then Mark would come along and carelessly swipe it away, destroying what she worked so hard for. But Mark's actions and attitude were more deliberate than a swipe, thought Meggie. It was like he was pulling on the last remaining loose thread of the only remnant of fabric to their marriage. As he yanked and tugged on the thread, it unraveled to a point where it was no longer recognizable. And irreparable. In this way, Meggie was unlike the spider. She had no idea where to even begin to start the spinning process.

Meggie apologized to the spider as she sipped her coffee.

"I'll never do that to you again," she said aloud.

****

So it was with a new purpose, and practically guilt-free, that Meggie put together the itinerary of homes to show Ryan. She had called him with the schedule, and had taken great pains to look, smell and feel her best on the day of their outing. She was wearing her most form-fitting and flattering bluejeans, and a super-soft cashmere sweater – a lime green, which was a very becoming color to her complexion, making her hazel eyes appear emerald-like. She had spritzed herself with some *Obsession*, a long-ago birthday gift from Mark, back when he had taken the time and made the effort to actually remember her birthday. Meggie was excited, but nervous. She hoped that neither sentiment would show.

He arrived at her office right at the appointed time – on the minute – *not* late. That alone was nice. He looked good, like maybe he had gone to a little trouble for her as well, with a crisp, clean and pressed polo, a pair of khakis, and slip-on docksiders. Why couldn't Mark have that kind of consideration for Meggie?

Ryan placed his hand on the small of her back as they made their way to the parking lot.

"Let's take my car," he said.

"But that's not necessary – I can drive."

"We may be doing a lot of driving around, Meg. I don't want to use up all your gas."

How thoughtful!

"Okay," she said, as he led her to his Jeep Cherokee. He opened the door for her, and then took it upon himself to fasten her in, leaning protectively and intimately over her as he clicked the buckle of her seat belt in place.

"You just tell me where to go, and I'll get us there," as he slid into the driver's seat.

Ryan had this very manly, take-charge way about him that Meggie found exceptionally appealing. She *liked* that he was taking control, even if it was just the driving. She gave him the first address.

"I love that neighborhood," he said.

"So do I."

They had walked through three of the seven houses on her list. To Meggie, it was feeling more like they were a married couple looking for their first home, rather than she an agent, and he the buyer. He kept asking her what she thought of every detail, as if all that mattered was that *she* be pleased. It was easy and fun to fall into this role playing – dangerous game that it was. How Meggie wished that she and Mark had had this kind of experience together. Moving into *his* house that he already owned and was living in had not been anything like this.

After the third house tour, Ryan announced that he was starved, and asked Meggie if he could take her to lunch.

So they went to *Apache Trout Grill*, an amazing spot overlooking the bay – the stunning view from this restaurant was unsurpassed, and the food was pretty incredible too. Another early morning rain had given way to a spectacularly resplendent day. Leaves were beginning to change color, and somehow everything looked more vivid – a deeper intensity and clarity – almost surreal. Autumn in Northern Michigan was an invigorating feast for the eyes, exquisite in its brilliant display.

Ryan took the liberty of ordering a Cosmopolitan Martini for her. It was a wonderful, refreshing choice -- just what she was craving. How did he know? Both Ryan and Meggie decided upon the Whitefish Sandwich, and placed their order. They chitchatted for awhile about the homes they'd seen, and then Ryan turned to gaze thoughtfully out the window.

"So, do you really *not* believe in God? asked Meggie, after the silence started becoming uncomfortable for her.

This quickly got his attention.

"No ... no, I'm just not *sure*," he explained. "I'm more like you. I suppose that if there *is* a God, and if that God created me, then he made me a doubting Thomas – so in a way, it's *His* fault that I'm not sure! *I yam what I yam!"* he mimicked Popeye, laughed, and then, "I do have more faith in God than I do in anything man-made, though. Including the Bible. And including organized religion."

Meggie laughed at his Popeye impersonation, but like with anyone willing to talk about it with her, she was anxious to get his "take" on God and religion.

"Oh I know! Some of the most corrupt people are actually religious leaders! Sometimes church seems like nothing more than a business," agreed Meggie. "Although they often do use their money to help people ..." she added.

"I'm not sure about that. I mean, look at the Catholic Church and all the opulence in The Vatican! In my humble opinion, anyone who chooses to go into the service of God should be living like the least of his brothers. And that goes for the leaders of any church or religious organization. That would only leave more to go where it's really needed. Not to mention they'd be setting an example."

"Yeah ... I agree. But as far as getting it to where it's really needed, it seems to go to those who know how to work the system, rather than the ones who are truly in need."

"In many ways, church is a lot like the government. Tithing is kinda like taxes. And there's a *lot* of waste!"

"Mark and I used to go to church. But I think I embarrassed him by asking too many difficult questions. They probably all thought I was a heathen or something. He sometimes still goes, but even he believes that spirituality comes from within. Organized religion always seems to provide some kind of disappointment. And I think you're right – it's that politics of organized religion that, once you're aware of, is such a turn-off."

"You know Meggie, once upon a time I was actually a Catholic. I even went to Catholic schools when I was a kid growing up in St. Louis."

"You're kidding! What happened?" she said this in such a way as to jokingly insinuate that he was now a heathen himself.

"I dunno. Ha! I was even an altar boy!"

"Wow. You were really into it then."

"Yeah, but it ended up badly."

"What do you mean?"

Ryan took a swig of his martini.

"I was kind of … *ousted*."

"What do you mean, ousted?"

Ryan snickered. "A corrupt priest sealed my doom."

"Okay. So tell me what happened already."

"I was fifteen years old, and had been an altar boy for two years. The guy who had been head altar boy for several years was going away to college, so they needed someone to take his place. I was a shoo-in, since I'd been doing it longer than anyone else. But there was one kid – kind of the priest's *pet*, if you know what I mean. He was only thirteen, and such a goody-two-shoes. I swear, in hindsight, I wonder what may have gone on behind those confessional doors … but anyway, he got it. I was so pissed. And so was my Dad. He beat the shit out of me, like it was my fault."

"You should say, *Merde,* instead of the sh- word," Meggie pointed out. For some reason she just hated blatant cussing, but at the same time understood the necessity of using those words at times. She continued the conversation, "So that doesn't explain why they ousted you."

"They ousted me because the priest got caught stealing the tithes. I was the one that reported him."

"That's insane! You were doing the right thing, and they ousted *you*?"

"Well … the priest ended up committing suicide. He hung himself."

"*Merde*! That's horrible!" she said, demonstrating how much more civilized it was to use French equivalents. "But that's not your fault! I don't get why they ousted you!"

"Here's the thing Meggie, and I have *never told a living soul about this till now*." Ryan stopped talking as if he were debating whether or not to proceed.

"*Tell* me!"

"I kind of set him up."

"What? You set up the priest?"

"Yeah."

"You mean he didn't steal the tithes?"

"Nope. I did."

"But then how come they thought he did?"

"Because I put the money in his drawer, and then reported that I saw him take it."

Meggie was dumbfounded.

"Why did you do that?"

"I told you, he passed me over for the head altar boy spot."

"Seriously? You did that to him because of *that*?"

Ryan drew in a deep breath and replied, "No, not entirely."

"What then?"

"He was messing with kids."

"You mean, like molesting?"

"Yeah."

"You?"

"Oh no. No, no, not me -- but the kid who got the head spot. Like I said, he was the favorite. There had to be a reason why."

"Did you know this for sure?"

"Some things you just know, Meggie. Yeah, I knew for sure. I don't know how I knew, but I knew. When that kid got my job, I absolutely knew what was going on. That's why I did it."

Their sandwiches were delivered at this point. Neither Ryan nor Meggie were particularly hungry anymore, but they dug in.

Meggie was quiet, taking all this in. Something wasn't ringing quite true about the story. Maybe Ryan had actually been molested by this priest but was too ashamed to admit it? That really could be the only reason Ryan would have done such a horrible thing. Frankly, Meg was surprised that Ryan was even telling her about this story.

"Your turn," said Ryan, with a note of teasing in his voice.

"What do you mean, *my* turn?"

"Well, this is kind of like, *truth or dare*, and I've volunteered a deep, dark, secret truth about myself. Now I want to know a deep, dark secret truth about you. That's how it works."

"I *know* how to play truth or dare! We just never established that we were playing that game! So you can't expect that from me – it's not fair." But even as she said this, she was filled with a thrill of clandestine self-exposure – the sense that they were stepping over a boundary that would forever connect them. A bond, like blood-brothers, or something. Suddenly, she felt like she was fifteen years old, playing spin-the-bottle. But this was not a game, and the secret she had to tell was a shameful, ugly truth. But it was a truth that she felt Ryan would understand – be accepting, rather than judgmental. Ryan was the first person Meggie had known that she could bare her soul to, without fear of repercussion. Or of being "ousted," she thought to herself.

"Meggie. Telling truths about each other is the way to a deeper, more meaningful friendship. I want that with you. I don't know why, but I feel a connection with you that I don't normally feel. I've felt it since day one." He gazed steadily at her as he spoke, making the words seem heartbreakingly heartfelt.

Meggie's secret had been one that she had been hungering to confide in someone about. She had always felt a sort of trepidation with Mark. Almost mistrust – not that he would betray her in any way, but that he would *judge* her – somehow make it her fault. Just like her mother had done. Since Mark was her only friend, it had left her with nobody to talk to – especially about *this*. Until now, Meggie had not even realized how desperately she had wanted to talk about it. Now, she had an invitation, no, almost more like a demand, to bare her soul. For some reason, Meggie felt that Ryan had not told her the whole truth about his incident with the priest. Maybe if she opened up to him, it would allow him the freedom to be entirely honest. She began tentatively,

"Well. Most of the time I block it out. In fact, I can't even remember a lot of it ..."

"I know *exactly* what you mean," he interrupted.

The interruption didn't faze Meggie. In fact, it made her more convinced of the fact that he hadn't been completely open about his ordeal. There was definitely a kinship here.

When she began to let it all out, it was like a floodgate opening up. At first she spoke with a detached kind of reporting of events, but as she went on her demeanor took on a trance-like modulation. If someone had been watching from another table, it would have looked like she had been hypnotized. Somehow, Ryan had managed to keep their martini glasses full without Meggie realizing it. She drank with a thirst that appeared unquenchable. Meggie just picked at her sandwich, while Ryan inhaled his.

Her tale began with when Larry-the-monster moved in with Meggie and her mother. They had only just met! Meggie was pretty sure that he had been homeless – perhaps thrown out of his last house and relationship. He had immediately taken on the role of "father" to Meggie, but not in a good way. He had assumed that she was a bad kind of girl, and likely prone to trouble. So his method was a sudden and irrational strictness, with the threat of some kind of punishment should Meggie step out of line at all. The thing was, Meggie was about the best kid that there ever could be. She didn't smoke, drink, party – for goodness sake, she didn't even have any friends to hang out or get into trouble with! Meggie's only friends were her books. Her only outings were to the library. But Larry treated her as though she was the worst kind of delinquent. And Meggie's mother encouraged his authoritarian strong-hold!

Meggie's mother worked the breakfast shift at Denny's. This meant that she left the house at 4:45 every morning to get to the store to get it ready to open by 6am. Meggie normally slept till about 7am in order to get to school by 7:45.

So when Larry began his early morning trips into Meggie's bedroom, she already had a very healthy fear of the man. He had craftily eased into his manipulative molestations. At first, he would lie next to her, kissing her cheek or rubbing her back and shoulders, and telling her that he was sorry for all the names he called her during daylight hours. He told her that he was just waiting for her to prove that she was actually a *good* girl. In Meggie's sleepy state, the shoulder and backrubs felt pretty good, which made her feel really weirded out. The confusion she had felt about *just* what Larry might be doing made her put up with it, in a stiff, but relenting way.

It had quickly progressed to very inappropriate touching, fondling, and then, finally, penetration. Meggie felt like a prisoner in her own bed. She was scared to death of Larry. She was also scared to death of her own mother. Larry had warned her that he would only tell her mother that Meggie had *invited* him in, had Meggie told her what was happening. And Meggie knew that her mother would believe him. In a way, Meggie even wondered if this was partially true, being that the initial backrubs had felt good. It made her believe that she was a disgusting tramp. Her hatred of Larry, and fear of his apparent power over them was paralyzing. Ironically, during the daylight hours, when Meggie's mother was there, Larry had done and about-face, and had almost been going overboard with kindness toward Meggie. He would tell her mother what a good girl she was. Instead of praising Meggie herself, her mother would respond in short, curt exclamations, like, "Well, well, isn't that nice?" It was more like jealousy than any kind of pride.

The situation was thoroughly dysfunctional and unbearable for Meggie.

Somewhere along the way during her narrative, Meggie had begun to cry. It was working its way into a sob, and so Ryan asked for the bill, paid it, and led Meggie out to the car.

When they got into the car, Ryan pulled Meggie over toward him and just held her. He gently stroked her hair, saying, "It's an impossible situation when somebody bigger, stronger, and more powerful than you takes advantage of that. And in your case, in the worst way. Meggie, it is not your fault. *It is not your fault.*"

Meggie slowly extricated herself from Ryan's embrace, and smiled weakly at him as she wiped her face and dripping nose on her sleeve. She took a deep breath and said,

"Well, I got him back. I killed him."

Now it was Ryan's turn to be dumbfounded.

"You … killed … *murdered* him?"

"I think so. I mean, I may have."

"How could you not *know*?"

"I smashed his head in with a baseball bat. It was one afternoon after I saw him hit my mother. Lord knows I had put up with his abusing me, sexually, for quite some time. But something in me snapped when I saw him hit her. And believe me, she did *not* deserve my defending her! In fact, after I knocked him flat, I was surprised that she didn't beat me. She was screaming at me, calling me horrible names. Names that made me realize that she had known all along what was going on in my bedroom in the early morning hours. She knew. And *I knew* she knew. And she knew that I knew that she knew! It was one of those terrible moments of clarity that reveal all the ugliness and torrid truth. She ran to help Larry, screeching at me the whole time. So I bolted. I ran away, never to return. I have never seen her, nor spoken to her, since. For all I know, she could be dead now too. She is to me anyway."

"Why do you think that you killed Larry?"

"The way the bat hit his skull. It had a sound that sounded like the word, *kill*. I did check the obituaries for weeks afterward, and never saw his name. I also called hospitals in the area to see if he had been admitted, but no, nothing … So I guess I'm not really sure that I killed him. Maybe a part of me just likes to think that. But he's dead to me anyway, just like my mother is."

"Wow. Where was your biological father in all this?"

"Are you kidding? My mother had absolutely no idea who my father might have been! I honestly think that she supplemented her Denny's income with a little bit of prostitution on the side."

"Oh my God, Meggie."

"Yeah, right, *oh my God*. Where was *He*? Really? *Where was He?* Or at least, where was my guardian angel? See? That's what I want to know! I prayed and prayed – and *nothing* – my prayers were ignored!"

"Oh Meg. I'm surprised you believe in God at all."

"Well I do. I don't understand Him, but I believe. You know, sometimes the things that may not even be true are the things that people need to believe in the most. It doesn't really matter if it's true or not – in fact, we may never know. What harm does it do to believe in God? Really? Can you think of *one* negative consequence to having that belief? That faith in something more powerful? To be accountable to? If everyone believed, and even *feared* God, just imagine what a better world this would be!"

"Touche', Meg."

Meggie was far too exhausted at this point to tell Ryan about her experience with her guardian angel, it would have to wait for another day, so instead she asked him to bring her back to the office so she could go on home. Although she didn't feel "drunk", she felt slightly nauseous, and so, *so* tired.

"We can pick up with the rest of the houses tomorrow. I'll notify the other agents of the change of plan. Is that okay?"

"Sure," he said. Ryan was subdued by Meggie's story and her painful past, and at the same time he was elated that she had opened up to him in this way. It solidified his resolve that they were meant to be together. Unlike Mark, Ryan would protect this delicate, beautiful bird.

****

A good night's sleep did much to rejuvenate Meggie. She slept more soundly that she had in months. Being able to *finally* tell someone her deep, dark secret had had some kind of cathartic effect. It was sort of like the reboot of someone's brain after they'd had a seizure. The sleep she experienced was like that strange, post-ictal sleep that generally follows seizure activity. Meggie only knew about this because her mom had suffered from occasional seizures when Meggie was a child. It had been frightening, but her mom had always seemed a little more clear-headed after one occurred.

This morning, Meggie felt clear-headed. She was looking forward to spending more time with Ryan. When she told Mark that she would be working with Ryan again all day, he said, and a bit sarcastically,

"So you didn't find him his dream-house yesterday?"

What was that? A tiny hint of jealousy? Mark's reaction made Meggie feel almost … imperious. He *should* feel jealous! He *deserves* to feel jealous! She thought to herself with a touch of giddiness, *how do you like them apples?*

"It may take awhile," she replied matter-of-factly, "which is fine with me – he's fun to hang around with."

"Well I'm glad you're having such a great time." But he didn't sound all that glad. "I've got to go in to the studio this morning. I'll see you later." As he walked out the back door, he shut it a little too briskly, which resembled a slam.

Veerrry interesting, thought Meggie, *the tables seem to be turning ... a bit of peripateia, I should say.*

When Ryan joined her an hour later at the office to begin another day of house-hunting, he seemed pensive. He had arrived somewhat early, so they decided to go have some coffee and muffins at *The TC Pie Company* before heading out.

They took a table by the window.

"So, are you excited about the houses we're going to see today?" asked Meggie. Ryan's quiet mood was making her feel a bit anxious. Did she make a mistake by opening up to him yesterday?

"Oh, yeah ... of course I am, Meg. I just ..."

"Just what?"

"I don't know ... yesterday was pretty heavy, don't you think?"

"I'm sorry. Maybe I shouldn't have laid all that on you."

"No! No, I'm *so* glad you did. It makes me feel very close to you. And very protective. I mean, I thought about it all night, Meg. If you didn't actually kill that guy, I'd want to go out and find him and do it myself!"

"That's not why I told you, Ryan. I don't want you to think about it like that."

"Why *did* you tell me?"

"I don't know … I guess I felt I could trust you with the information. That you wouldn't judge me. That you'd understand somehow."

"Does Mark know?"

"Are you kidding? Mark would definitely not understand. He would probably blame *me* …"

"Well I *do* understand, and like I said yesterday, it was *not your fault*. Meggie, I am so … *overwhelmed* that you trust me enough to be so open and honest. I will never let you down. Never. And I will always be here for you."

Meggie was starting to feel sort of awkward. Where do you go after you've bared your soul the way she did … the way they *both* did yesterday? She wanted to get back on solid ground somehow, but wasn't sure how to go about it. It was like they had been too intimate, too fast. She sipped on her coffee and picked at her muffin nervously, while Ryan gazed steadily at her.

"Stop staring at me," she said, but with a self-conscious smile.

"I'm sorry. I can't help it." Ryan shifted his focus to look out the window at the parking lot. Minutes passed, and Meggie became aware of the blurred chatter at the tables around them.

Ryan's voice emerged from the animated background yakkety yak,

"Meggie," he whispered softly.

She waited, holding her breath apprehensively.

He slowly drew his gaze from the window, and looked determinedly into Meggie's eyes, his own warm, brown eyes slightly magnified by his glasses' lens. It had a Mr. MaGoo effect, despite the seriousness of Ryan's demeanor. Meggie wasn't sure, but they also appeared a bit moist. It was almost comical, and Meggie had to stifle a laugh.

He continued, "You know, I don't know if you are truly the *most beautiful* woman I have ever seen in my life, or if it's just because ..."

She waited, suddenly nervous again.

"Meggie," he repeated.

She went ahead and laughed, and turned pink as she did so.

"*What?*"

"Oh ... nothing ..." as he reverted his gaze toward the cars again.

Part of Meggie wanted to push it further. There was no doubt that this kind of adoration and complimentary commentary was stoking her self-esteem. And her poorly bruised ego was practically ravenous for this kind of attention. But it was like the light had suddenly turned red, indicating a sure collision had she tried to run it. So she changed the subject. But the words had been said. There they were, out of his mouth – big and bold, daring and splendid. *She was the most beautiful woman he had ever seen!* They played over and over in the background of her inconsequential prattle as she began to talk about the houses they'd be looking at today, and then went into her spiel about the merits of home ownership. *What else could she talk about safely*? But Ryan never stopped looking out the window, like his feelings had been hurt or something.

She was at a loss as to what to say to calm the situation, and made an attempt to gently tease him, saying in a goofy voice, "You … *dingleberry!"*

This seemed to bring him out of his sullen whatever-it-was.

"Dingleberry? Did you just call me a *dingleberry?"* he laughed, and added, "You know, you just reminded me of Kathy Bates' character in *Misery*! That's a word she would have used!"

"Oh *please*, don't compare me to her – that's scary!" The thick tension was momentarily suspended – thank goodness.

"There is *nothing* miserable about you, Miss Meg! Now don't you have something to show me?"

"Four more houses to go!" she announced a little too brightly, grateful that the conversation had become light again, as Ryan paid their tab.

"Let's get to it, then!" Ryan returned with an enthusiasm tinged with what vaguely sounded like disappointment. The air was somehow charged with unspoken words that Ryan seemed to be having a great deal of trouble holding in. It was as if he was unsure whether or not Meggie was ready to hear what he would like to say, what he was obviously *dying* to say, which had to be the source of the disappointment she sensed. This was how perceptive Meggie was – because it was true.

Those unspoken words followed them out to the car, and then hung in the air there in the enclosed space. Both Meggie and Ryan tried to ignore them. They arrived at the next house on her list. Fortunately, the listing agent was there to show them around and answer any questions they might have. This gave them a temporary barrier of protection from each other.

When they climbed back into the car, *there were those unspoken words again* – more insistent this time, but remaining mute for the time being.

The next house was one of Meg's favorites. She didn't even have to verbally express this, as it was written all over her face. Her ardor for the place did not get lost on Ryan.

"Whoa!" he said as they walked slowly through the rooms, sunshine pouring through the tall, crystal-clear windows encased in gorgeous, natural woodwork and casting beams of gleaming light to bounce off the polished wood floors.

"*This* may be the one," he continued, looking intently at Meggie.

"I love this house," was all she could manage.

"You *love* this house, Meggie?" He held out his hand to her, beckoning her, "Come here."

As she moved tentatively toward him, he reached out to grasp her hands, pulling her in. She allowed herself to be engulfed in his arms, embraced in a way that she could not remember having been held in an eternity.

She was acutely aware of his skin, his scent, his warmth, her body quickly tuning in to every ripple of muscle, the valleys and hills of his firm flesh, and the rapidly growing mound that was pressing urgently against her. He whispered savagely into her ear, his breath hot,

"Move into this house with me, Meggie … Can't you see? I am *violently* in love with you!"

His words were all at once an irresistible aphrodisiac, while at the same time a serpentine poison.

Meggie felt flummoxed and flustered. Deep inside, she had been expecting this, *hoping* for this … but now, the reality of it was throwing her entirely off balance.

The next thing she knew, he was kissing her, passionately and frantically.

She kissed him back as her own body responded treasonously. She was experiencing a desire that would forsake her caution, throwing it recklessly to the wind.

He led her into the master bedroom, where the owner had foolishly placed a thick, luxurious wall-to-wall carpet over hardwood. He gently eased her to that floor, and then cradled her in his strong, Adonis-like arms.

"I love you, Meggie. I *love* you."

"Ryan ... what about *Whitney*? Aren't you planning to marry *her*?"

"Jesus, Meggie – surely you know better than that. I only took her out to throw Mark off the scent. He was definitely starting to act suspicious ... *you* are the one I love. You are the only one I want."

Mark was acting suspicious? Is that why he suddenly seemed a little on the insecure side? Meggie unanticipatedly and inappropriately felt sorry for Ryan. It was an unexpected emotion that simply overtook her without warning. Her sympathy had to do with unrequited love. She didn't love Ryan. She didn't want him to love her. Meggie loved Mark! But Mark didn't love Meggie! What kind of a ludicrous *Bob and Carol and Ted and Alice* situation had she gotten herself into?

She wrapped her arms around his neck, almost charitably, but with a touch of resolved intent; however ... she couldn't go through with it. Her body once again betrayed her, as the previously felt desire was promptly replaced with unforeseen revulsion.

Ryan took her embrace as a full-steam-ahead acquiescence. Permission and consent granted. He ground himself vigorously against her, slipping his hand under her sweater.

Meggie still hadn't spoken. Her mind began to play tricks on her, Ryan's unabating and immediate anatomy transposed with images from Meggie's sordid past. These images flashed intermittently, fleetingly, and almost imperceptively behind her tightly closed eyes. The terror that she felt was unreasonable as Ryan continued to take her. Her jeans were unbuttoned, pulled down, and then pushed to her ankles by Ryan's feet, which had *somehow* become bare, as he had from the waist down. Her underwear followed. She couldn't keep up with the events as they unfolded. It was like she was observing after the fact, rather than a participant. Her crazed fear was paralyzing her.

She finally found her voice,

"No ... no," she faltered weakly.

All of a sudden, Ryan was no longer there. In his place, the hulking, menacing shape of Larry-the-monster took form.

Meggie let out a scream that would have woken the dead.

This had the effect of pouring a bucket of ice over Ryan. He abruptly halted his amorous persistence. He had a look of complete shock and confusion on his face as he blurted out,

"Oh my God! I'm sorry Meggie! I'm so sorry! I thought this was what you *wanted*. I'm *so* sorry!" He fumbled away from her, snatching his clothing from the floor and stumbling back into them.

Meggie shakily and clumsily pulled her own clothing back into place.

"It's not you, Ryan. It's me. I thought it was what I wanted … but I can't. I can't do this. I'm sorry … I'm sorry. I'm married. And I love Mark." Her voice had that stale, smacky kind of quality that came from a profoundly dry mouth – a fight or flight response under extreme duress.

"Honestly, Meg. I thought you wanted this. I thought you wanted *me*. And Mark treats you like *shit*!"

"I *know* that! Look … I just want to go home."

Ryan was only too anxious to high-tail it out of there, in case any neighbor or passer-by had heard Meggie's scream and called the police. He couldn't get her back to her office fast enough.

****

It wouldn't be that difficult to lie to Mark. She had, after all, been lying to him since the day she met him – sort of. Not telling the whole truth was more like telling a white lie than a flat-out falsehood, wasn't it? The thing is, Meggie *wanted* to tell him the truth – the whole truth, and nothing but the truth.

When she got home that afternoon, Mark wasn't there. She debated whether or not to call him at the studio, asking him to come home early so they could talk. But the memory of how he reacted when she mentioned going to counseling kept her from picking up the phone. What she *really* wanted was for Mark to initiate the conversation they so badly needed to have. That would show her that he truly cared. For *her* to initiate it made her feel like she was groveling or something.

Poor Ryan, she thought. She hadn't meant to lead him on, but that's what happened. But *he* had started it all! That very first day when he came to the house – Meggie had never before seen such blatant flirtation, especially with her being the recipient of it! The attention had gone straight to her head in a major way. She encouraged it, and now in hindsight, had used Ryan to make Mark jealous. But no, it was more than that. She *had* been attracted to him. And she had felt a connection which allowed her to finally open up to someone. The problem was, it was the wrong person. *Maudit! Maudit! Maudit!*

The sense of rejuvenation and clear-headedness that Meggie had just experienced that morning had turned into an overwhelming lethargy. A dense fog had somehow settled around her brain, making simple thought difficult. The only thing she could see with any clarity came to her involuntarily like flashing polaroids or snapshots of those previously blocked out memories of Larry. Talking about it with Ryan had been like opening Pandora's box.

Meggie had always convinced herself that she was unaffected by her childhood, and that the ordeal she'd suffered at Larry's man-hands was one that she had successfully buried. Now, as it seemed, the whole hideous reality of it had only been covered by a scab that she had allowed to heal improperly, forming a crusty, hardened mass. Her encounter with Ryan had ripped the scab right off, exposing the gaping, bleeding hole beneath it. As the horrendous details continued to reveal themselves to Meggie, she was shocked by her ability to just squelch them for so long – just moving through life, *La-Te-Da* without giving it a smidgeon of thought. But now her mind was obsessing over it, and her thoughts were making her sick to her stomach.

She fell asleep before Mark came home, and then she slept … and slept … and slept. Mark didn't wake her. The next morning she woke up in a panic – the sheets stuck to her clammy, perspiring body.

"*Geez*, Meg, are you alright?"

As it dawned on her that she had only been dreaming, she began to feel some relief, but at the same time she couldn't help still feeling upset.

"I was having a dream – *a nightmare* – about *you*. I was out in the middle of nowhere – some horrible neighborhood with druggies and thugs hanging around. You were supposed to pick me up, but you forgot and just left me there …"

"So you *wake up* pissed at me … no wonder …"

"I'm not pissed at you, Mark. It was just a dream." But in truth, she *was* pissed at him, for leaving her in that dangerous, awful neighborhood there in the dream, and for so much more. So she added, "But you know, dreams *mean* something. Sometimes they help us to work something out, like a problem you're having trouble dealing with … or they bring something up from your subconscious that might be bothering you and you're not even *aware* of it."

"So which is it in this case? Do you feel I've abandoned you, or let you down, or put you in danger somehow?"

Meggie was quiet for a minute or two, then ventured, "Mark, I don't want to fight, but it seems like I can't even tell you how I'm feeling about things without you getting all mad or storming off. You never even want to discuss it. I'm *afraid to answer* your question!"

They lay there, side by side, looking up at the ceiling. Mark finally spoke,

"You sure slept a long time."

"I know. And I'm *still* tired."

"Meggie, I've been thinking about what you said about us getting some counseling …"

Meggie's breath caught in her throat as a sudden, unexpected sob escaped. Mark turned over toward her and leaned up on his elbow so that he could see her face.

"I don't want to be the kind of husband whose wife can't talk to him. I think I just try to avoid conflict at all costs – even if it means not listening to you. I mean, do I *do* that?"

"Yeah, Mark, you do."

"Well, I don't want to be like that, Meg. I'm willing to see someone if that's what you think we need. But honestly, I'd much rather work out our issues between ourselves."

"We definitely have a few."

They both laughed half-heartedly, and Mark lay back down on the pillow, both looking up at the ceiling again. Meggie couldn't help herself, and began to cry quietly at Mark's side.

Mark finally spoke again, very gently, very softly.

"I need to ask you something, and I want you to be honest."

Meggie looked over at him as salty tears trickled down the sides of her face.

"Are you and Ryan having an affair?"

She bolted upright. "*No!* No, we're not! Why would you ask that?"

"Whoa … whoa … Meg, none proclaim their innocence so loudly as the guilty ..."

"I'm *not* guilty, Mark. I'm just surprised that you would ask that – or *think* that! Ryan is *your* friend, and to me he's … he's a *client*, I guess."

"I don't know, Meg. Something doesn't feel right. The guy has had a thing for you since the day he met you – don't think I haven't noticed. He's made it pretty obvious. The thing is, even if I *don't* trust him, I've always trusted you. But now you're spending time alone together … and suddenly you're acting funny. Something's wrong."

"Mark, I'm only acting funny because something's wrong with *us*. In fact, I won't be working with Ryan anymore anyway. The prices of the homes he liked were more than he had anticipated, so he decided to wait."

"Really?"

"Yeah."

"Well, when he decides to look again, I'd prefer he find another agent."

"Fine by me."

Both Mark and Meggie were quite aware that their conversation wasn't entirely an honest one. But they continued to lie there in stillness, both lost in their thoughts, doubts, suspicions and unasked questions. Nothing could have spoken so loudly as the silence hanging in the air between them. Neither dared to venture an utterance, lest they betray themselves, and the omissions and half truths they had been living.

****

The last class of the day began at 11am sharp. Mark was already worn out, having lifelessly muddled through the 7am and 9am classes. He didn't know why, but he was surprised when Ryan showed up, ready and raring to go as usual. Whitney had stopped coming to class after the disastrous double-date. No surprise there. Mark did not miss her attention-seeking and distracting *look-at-me, look-at-me* behavior. Ryan gave him a curt salute, and the work-out began. Seeing Ryan gave Mark a burst of angry fuel, for which he was actually grateful. After 45 minutes of going through routines and fight patterns, Mark announced that they would spend the last 15 minutes of class sparring. The class paired up, leaving Mark and Ryan to spar against each other, as the "Mark and Ryan team" was now long established, and frankly, nobody really wanted to go against either man – even if just for fun.

Mark and Ryan faced each other, arms and fists in position, and wordlessly began to jab and kick, circling like two stalking tigers in a cage. When contact was made, it was not with the usual controlled type of sparring blows, but with a more vigorous force that declared the smoldering animosity between them. After ten minutes, they had worked up quite a sweat, and both were feeling the bruises that would show up, dark purple and mottled, later. Mark leaned back and to the side, and swept out his right leg for a powerful roundhouse kick. Ryan, quick on his feet, dodged the attack by jumping slightly back and to the right, lowering his head as he bent to avoid the impact.

Wrong thing to do. Mark, with his leg still in the air, then snapped his lower leg backward, catching Ryan square on the temple with his heel. Ryan fell to the mat, stunned. Mark then leaned over him and said in a fierce whisper, "Stay away from my wife."

He then abruptly announced that class was over, and instead of his customary waiting by the door to bow to each student, he went into his office and shut the door.

Ryan was not about to let it go. He followed Mark out and yanked the door open.

"What the hell is *your* problem?" he asked, loudly enough that the departing students heard him, and very quickly and uneasily shuffled out of the studio.

"I think it's time you find another class."

"What the hell? What did *I* do?"

"I want you to leave my wife alone. Stop *weaseling* your way into our lives! She wants *nothing* to do with you."

"You don't know what the hell you're talking about! You don't even *know* your own wife! Newsflash, buddy – Meggie and I have a connection – a bond that you, or anyone else, can't break."

"You must be insane! What kind of a *connection* could you *possibly* have with *my* wife? You're delusional, man!"

"Yeah? Delusional? *Your wife* confided her childhood past to *me* – something she can't talk to *you* about! *You're* the one who doesn't know what the hell he's talking about!

You don't even know that your *own wife* was sexually abused when she was a kid! Meggie doesn't *trust* you enough to open up to you. And how long have you been married? Oh yeah ... I'm delusional alright. It's *me* she confides in. *It's me she trusts!"*

Mark was completely thrown off guard. What on earth was Ryan talking about? Was he lying, or did Meggie really tell him what he was saying she told him? He struggled to regain some semblance of composure, but underneath was ready to strangle this bespectacled moron. He couldn't ever remember feeling such hatred and contempt toward another human being in his life.

He walked stiffly, exercising great restraint, around his desk, opened the door to show Ryan out, and said forcefully,

"Get out. And don't come back. And for your information, I know everything there is to know about my wife."

Ryan shoved up against Mark as he walked past him, who stood as solid as a granite statue, and hissed as he went out the door,

"You're an *asshole.*"

Mark slammed the door behind him, catching the shocked and alarmed glimpse of skinny Bernard, the last student to leave the building.

****

Ryan foolishly drove right over to Mark and Meggie's house. He found her in the backyard, playing with Mel and Houdini. She turned around when she heard him say her name, and froze.

"Where's Mark?" she asked with confused concern in her voice.

"Meggie. We need to talk. And we need to talk *now*, before Mark gets here."

"But I don't *want* to talk. We have nothing to talk about. Ryan, you need to leave."

"I'm not going anywhere, Meggie, until you admit how you feel."

"Admit how I *feel*?"

"I *know* how you feel. I know that you're trapped. Meggie. You should be with *me*, not that asshole who treats you like dirt."

"Mark doesn't treat me like dirt!"

"You *know* he does! How can you deny that? Meggie ... look ... just come away with me. Leave Mark. He doesn't love you. *I do*. And I know that deep down you love me."

"Ryan," she began to laugh nervously, "I don't know what to say, but you're wrong. I *do* love Mark. And he *does* love me. I am sorry ... really sorry, that you misread me, but you've got it all wrong. You really should go. Please. I'm begging you to just go."

Ryan stood there and looked like a child who might burst into tears because his favorite toy was just taken away.

She repeated, with more urgency, "*Please* go!"

He took a step toward her, then thought the better of it, and replied in a shaky voice,

"Okay, I'll go now. But I'm going to wait for you, Meggie. I know what's true. And I know you – better than you know yourself. You'll come around, and you know what? I'll *be* there, waiting."

And with that he turned and jogged back to his car, leaving Meggie dumbfounded, and a little scared.

****

Mark pulled into the driveway mere minutes after Ryan had squealed out. He strode straight up to Meggie, who watched with eyes widened as he ascended upon her. She was unsure if Mark and Ryan had passed each other on the road, or what. As Mark got within touching distance of Meg, he reached out and took her by the arm.

"Come with me, Meg. We need to talk."

He wasn't rough, but determined. She followed as he led her into the house, where they sat down together at the kitchen table. Meg just stared at him, waiting to see what was going to come out of his mouth.

"Meg ... were you *abused* in any way, like *sexually*, when you were a child?"

Meg's eyes grew even rounder, and her face began to get hot and pink.

"I ... ummm ... did Ryan tell you that?"

"I think the question is, did *you* tell *Ryan* that?"

Meggie looked down at her hands, which she had begun to twist around each other self-consciously.

"Mark," she began, "... it was a long time ago. I had kind of buried the whole thing – I never really felt comfortable talking about it."

"Until now? And with *Ryan*?"

Meggie began to cry, but it was not working as far as making Mark feel sympathy, regardless of the subject matter. He was too hurt to know that she had confided something so incredibly personal with that jerk – and not with *him*!

"I don't know, Mark ... we were just talking ... he ... he confided something very similar in *his* past to me, and then mine just sort of ... *came out*!"

Mark sat there, unmoving, staring at her with a look of disbelief and anguish on his face, and then he dropped his head into his hands and shook it slowly back and forth.

"I honestly don't know how you could have let yourself get so *intimate* with that *creep*. This feels like just as much a betrayal as it would have if you'd actually admitted to having an affair with him."

Meggie was starting to get mad as she realized that Mark was only looking at it, selfishly as usual, from his own perspective.

"Mark! Listen to yourself! All you care about is how it affects *you* that I told someone *other than you*! Can't you see? That's exactly why I could never tell you! You are always the victim, and I'm always the bad guy! I don't know how you manage to *always* turn it around that way. You're so judgmental – and *that's* why I couldn't tell you!"

"How on earth could I have seen you as the "bad guy" in that kind of situation? How would I have possibly *judged* you? You are *so wrong* about that! Meggie – why didn't you tell me about it? What a horrible thing to go through! And you know, I'm sorry if it bothers me that you told Ryan, but *how could it not?*"

"You *are* judgmental Mark. You always have been. I've been scared to death to reveal anything to you that might be considered *unworthy* of you in some way. *Oh high and mighty Mark.* You always blame me for being *insecure* when I speak up about your flirtations! *Pour le Dieu!* How do you think that makes me feel? Don't you think that when you flirt with other women it *creates* insecurity for me? I don't flirt with other men!"

"No, you just tell them your deepest, darkest secrets, and leave me out in the cold!"

"You can't seem to understand why I found it necessary to keep you 'out in the cold', can you? I don't know, Mark. What do you want me to tell you? Ryan was listening. He was compassionate ... and most of all, he didn't *judge* me! In hindsight, I wish I hadn't confided in him. It's pretty obvious that I couldn't, and *shouldn't have* trusted him. I am sorrier than you know about that."

Mark stood up from the table.

"I need to think about all this, Meg. Let me go up and take a shower, and then let's eat some lunch and talk more about this afterward. Okay?"

"Yeah ... okay." Meggie's emotions were all jumbled up. She was anxious, yet dreading this conversation, but knew it was necessary. Maybe this would be the turning point in their marriage – but the question remained, in which direction?

****

It is truly amazing how food can soothe the savage beast. Mark and Meggie managed to devour their grilled tuna and cheese sandwiches, which Meggie had fried up in a ton of butter, served with cinnamon-spiced applesauce. They were drinking hot Chamomile and Passionflower tea, as the cool autumn air and their frayed nerves called for something both warm and calming. Mark, being the reasonable guy that he was, had insisted that they eat lunch before "getting into it".

As they finished up, Meggie stood to pick up their plates, but Mark stopped her by grabbing her hand.

"Leave them, Meggie. Let's talk."

Although it was a bit disconcerting to Meg to sit at a table with dirty plates sitting right in front of them, she sat, but neatly piled them up, spreading their napkins over the top to hide the food remnants from view, and then pushed them to the far edge of the table. Mark chuckled under his breath as he watched.

"See? That's one of the things I love about you. You always like things *just-so*, and I have always been a beneficiary of your obsessive neat-freak nature ..."

Meggie smiled at the compliment, and was glad to hear Mark express some appreciation for her fastidious and particular ways. So often she had felt it went completely unnoticed. Neither of them realized just how much

Meggie's attempts to "hide the mess" actually *said* about her.

"I'd like to start, Meg, because I've done a lot of soul-searching over the past few weeks – at least since you mentioned going to counseling ..."

Meggie waited, *very* anxious to hear what Mark had to say, and still feeling reticent about what she was *willing* to say.

"First, I want to talk about how any perceived flirtation on my part might be affecting you."

"Perceived? You mean, it's all in my head, *perceived*?"

Please, oh please, thought Meggie, *don't let this be that kind of conversation, where it all gets turned around to me again* ...

"No. No, not at all. That's not what I meant. Meggie ... it has only been recently ... because of Ryan actually, and all the attention he's been giving you. Which honestly I didn't mind so much – until I began to think that it meant more to you than just ... *attention*."

"Go on ..."

Mark took a deep breath, his disjointed sentences proof that he was having difficulty verbalizing his thoughts and feelings.

"I don't think I really understood before how my actions, innocent as they were, affected you – made you feel insecure. And it wasn't *you*, it was because of *me*."

Meggie couldn't quite believe what she was hearing Mark say, and wanted to chime in with all her, *see? I told you so all along* comments, but she bit her tongue and waited for him to continue, while on the inside her heart was soaring.

"I guess I'm trying to apologize, Meg. Whatever's been going on between you and Ryan has made *me* feel insecure. *And I don't like it.* I suppose the shoe is on the other foot now. It's made me realize what you've been telling me for so long. I know I'm a flirt. I don't know why I do it, but Meg, I don't mean anything by it!"

Meggie looked down at her mug and traced the rim with her finger. Part of her wanted to lash out with an air of vindication. But she really couldn't believe that Mark was *finally* taking responsibility for the insecurity he had always accused her of, and that he had caused in the first place. *And* that he was admitting to feeling insecure because of Ryan! *Ha!* But she held these emotions in check, not wanting to break the generous spell Mark was under. It almost had a sense of a "fishing expedition" where Mark was manipulating her into revealing an affair between herself and Ryan. She wanted to be sure that his words were honest and heartfelt. She desperately needed for his words to be honest and heartfelt!

"I don't know why you do it, either, Mark. Especially knowing that it hurts me."

"Meggie – I *don't* want to hurt you! That's why I'm talking about this now. I just didn't realize how it made you feel, regardless of your telling me. I don't know, maybe I'm dense or something. Or maybe it was my way of keeping you an arm's length away. Maybe *I* was afraid of getting hurt. Of getting too close. I don't know, Meg ... I don't know."

"How were you afraid I might hurt you?"

"That maybe you'd go away ... that I might lose you or something, and that if I kept a certain distance it wouldn't hurt so badly? Honestly, I'm trying to figure it out myself. Like I said, I've been doing a lot of soul searching, and it ain't been too pretty."

Meggie wanted to laugh at his intentional poor grammar, but didn't have the heart. She knew that he was attempting levity, but this was no laughing matter.

"So where do we go from here, Mark?"

"Can we start fresh? Like today is the first day of the rest of our lives? That's what I'd like, Meg. And I'm really, really, *really* going to make an effort to consider your feelings before I say or do, or *don't do*, anything. Cause I know that *that* drives you crazy too."

Now Meggie *could* laugh. How true that was!

"So you'll put the toilet seat down after you use it?"

"Yes."

"And you'll take out the trash without my having to ask?"

"Yes."

"And you'll remember my birthday … and our anniversary?"

"I will do my best."

"And you'll *stop* ogling other women – and not just when I'm around, but *all the time*?"

"Meggie, now that I am truly aware of the damage it does, I will make every effort to never do that again. You really are the most beautiful woman in the world to me. I guess I just need to let you know more often."

"Wow, Mark. Talking about it like this makes it seem that our problems are not insurmountable after all … I'm wondering what *I* need to change to make *you* happy?"

"Just be open and … *honest*."

"I've always tried to be. Do you think I haven't?"

"Well … you never told me about your childhood."

"And you have always refused to talk about your parents! We have *never* talked about the Christmas fiasco! You have no idea how that affected me!"

Meggie's voice had gone up an octave or two – both were getting a little defensive.

"And I don't think you've told me the whole story with regard to Ryan … *have* you?"

So it *was* a fishing expedition. *This* was what was first and foremost on Mark's mind. He had said that he had always trusted Meggie, but it sure wasn't sounding like it.

"Okay," as she let out an exasperated breath.

"Okay what?"

"Yes, he made a pass."

"What do you mean, he made a pass?" Mark was trying, with great difficulty, to sound passive. To sound … civilized.

"Well … he … *kissed* me."

"He *kissed* you? And what did *you* do?"

Meggie was unsure of how honest she should be. She recognized the haughty tone coming through in Mark's voice. It was like a warning bell. He always sounded this way when he just *knew* he was right about something – even when he was *wrong*. She weighed the progress that they were apparently making against the possibility that her honesty could backfire, and ultimately decided to go for the gusto. Let's get it all – *everything* – out in the open. After all, how could they "start fresh" if they didn't wipe the slate clean?

"You know, at first … I *kind* of kissed back —-"

"God damn it, Meggie – you fricking kissed him *back*!?* What the hell *else* did you do?"

"You need to calm down if you want to talk about this, Mark. You either want me to be honest about this, or your temper is going to make me want to shut up about it. Which do you want? You want to start fresh or not?"

"Fine. Okay. I'm calm. Just tell me everything, Meggie." But even as he spoke those words, he maintained that aura of well-controlled rage. It was the way he sounded if anyone contradicted his religious beliefs. But they *had* to get through this ... and *past* it!

"Okay," she continued, with a touch of trepidation, "so after he kissed me, he kind of lowered me down on the floor."

"Go on." Mark's eyes were glaring as he attempted to keep his countenance cool and ambiguous.

Meggie was oblivious to the rumbling of the volcanic activity happening within her husband. She was too preoccupied with the events she was recounting, choosing her words carefully. It was strange, but even though these events were so recent, she was having a hard time remembering how they went down.

"I don't know how," she continued quietly, "but somehow my pants were pulled down –"

"WHAT?"

"I said NO, Mark. I told Ryan *no*! But he didn't seem to hear me ... until I *screamed*. Then he stopped."

"So you didn't –?"

"NO!"

"Where the hell *were* you when this took place?"

"At one of the empty houses I was showing him."

"God damn it, Meggie. Then what happened?" Mark's face had turned a deep purple, and his breathing was somewhat erratic. Meggie's own breathing was labored, and she had broken out in an uncomfortable perspiration.

"He took me right back to the office. We haven't spoken since – I mean, only once, and only for a minute."

"When was that? What do you mean, *only for a minute*? What did you say?" Mark was practically shouting at this point. Little bits of spit were flying out of his mouth. He had never before raised his voice in this way to Meggie. She might have been frightened, if the look on his face hadn't been one of pure and anguished heartbreak.

"Mark, please. Ryan believes he has strong feelings for me. He actually thinks he *loves* me." At this she laughed nervously.

"It's not fricking funny, Meg. You're a *married* woman. Is he fricking insane? So when did you talk to him again?"

"I don't know, maybe he is insane. Anyway, he stopped here just before lunchtime, before you got home. I told him that I am *in love with my husband*, and asked him to leave."

Mark didn't seem to hear the words Meggie spoke about being in love with him, he was too wrapped up in everything else.

"I'm going to *kill* that bastard." And with that, Mark got up from the table and walked out.

****

Where on *earth* is he going? And what is he going to do? Meggie was beside herself. She had *never* seen Mark in such a state. He always maintained composure. He was a control-freak to the *max* – especially when it came to his own reactions to things. But now … Meggie was very worried, to say the least. Mark was *out of control*. He was most likely on his way to Ryan's house. Meggie needed to do something, before something really bad happened.

So she called Ryan.

He answered the phone on the first ring, voice mistakenly full of anticipatory hope,

"Meggie?"

"Yes, Ryan, it's me. Ryan, *listen*. Mark is on his way to see you."

"Mark is on his way *here*? Why?"

"Ryan, I'm sorry – but I've told Mark everything that happened between you and me. *Everything*. He's not coming over to be sociable, I assure you."

"Jesus, F'ing Christ, Meg! Why did you do that? Do you want us to *fight* over you, is that it? A duel? Well, if that's what you want, *that's* what you'll get." And then he slammed down the receiver.

Meggie just stood there with the dead phone in her hand.

What have I done now?

****

Ryan's mind was spinning, formulating a plan – a plan to get rid of Mark, once and for all. The plan *could* backfire though, which meant that Ryan *might* get hurt – or worse. He went into his bedroom, carrying a dish towel. Using it as a barrier, he pulled a semi-automatic pistol from the bottom drawer of his bedside table. The gun was not registered – never had been. Ryan had purchased it, with cash, at an underground market he had discovered while on a trip to Atlanta. Although he hadn't had the opportunity to use it yet, he kept it fully loaded – *just in case*. He used the towel to wipe the gun clean, polishing it up to a dull glow. He carried it into the kitchen, and set it down on the butcher-block bar that served as his dining table.

All of a sudden, there was a loud and insistent pounding on the front door. Although he was expecting it, he was startled, and jerked in response as he heard Mark's voice from the other side of the door,

"Open the God-damned door you *asshole,* before I break it down!"

Ryan lived in a building that was a combination of condominiums and apartments. They were all townhouse configuration, which meant that Ryan had neighbors on either side, but none above or below him. As Mark stood there, shaking the door handle, banging on the door, and shouting at Ryan, the neighbor to the left cracked his door open to look curiously and apprehensively at who was making all that racket. Mark glanced over at him and stupidly explained to the neighbor,

"This *jerk* made a pass at *my* wife."

The neighbor very quickly shut his door again. While this brief exchange was taking place, Ryan had opened his own front door, and had already retreated to the kitchen area, expecting Mark to follow, which he did.

Ryan thought to himself, *Neighbor sees Mark – check one!*

Ryan leaned up against the sink with his muscular arms folded over his chest. He had a ridiculous goofy grin on his face, which infuriated Mark to no end.

As Mark stepped into the kitchen, his attention was caught by the metal-grey patina of the gun, right there in front of him on the counter.

He reached out and grabbed the weapon, and pointed it at Ryan's head. His hand and voice shook almost violently as he said,

"How I'd love to pull this trigger right now."

Ryan thought to himself, *Mark's prints on the gun – check two!*

"Go ahead, Mark. I honestly don't give a shit if you do. If I can't be with Meggie, then I don't even want to *live*. So fucking *pull the trigger!*"

Mark looked at Ryan as if he were some strange, alien creature, and shook his head like he couldn't quite believe what he was looking at, or what was happening. Ryan's glasses were a little fogged up, and he was still smirking that incredibly goofy grin, with a touch of self-satisfaction. It would have been almost comical had Mark not been seething with fury.

"You *are* insane. There is something *very wrong* with you, you know that Ryan? *You're a fricking lunatic.*"

He put the gun very gingerly back down on the butcher-block counter, and backed slowly toward the door, which he had left partially open. He wasn't *about* to turn his back on this crazed, maniacal clown. He felt for the handle, stepped back over the threshold, and pulled the door shut, exhaling a deep breath of pent-up tension, and then ran to his car as that very same neighbor watched from behind the curtain. He didn't hear the gunshot *pop* as he pulled out of the parking lot, tires burning rubber.

****

The agitated nervous energy that overcame Ryan after Mark's abrupt departure was making him feel almost intoxicated. The "plan" had been derailed, but not entirely. Ryan didn't *really* want to die, though he had been willing to, if it meant that Mark would rot in jail for the rest of his life. He could've placed a bet that Mark would be too whimpy to pull the trigger. The future, for all of them, was now in Ryan's hands.

He picked up the gun, again using the dish towel as a barrier, and pointed the barrel at his temple. This would truly be the end, he thought, and then he would miss out on comforting the inmate's lonely spouse. He had broken out in a profuse sweat, and was practically hyperventilating. He pictured the bullet slicing through his skull, pulverizing the grey matter, which caused him to drop the barrel down toward his abdomen instead. He then began to visualize his guts, colon and all, spilling out to the floor in a pulsating mass. Wouldn't that mean he'd have to live with a colostomy bag for the rest of his life? So he dropped the barrel again, just a notch. *STOP THINKING AND JUST DO IT!*

He pulled the trigger, the cloth of the towel pulling ever so slightly at the pressure.

Check three … he thought as his legs gave out.

Ryan felt as though he would pass out from the searing, burning pain that tore through his flesh.

The towel and gun fell to the floor alongside him, and he watched it fall, as if in slow motion. Blood had splattered all over the towel in such a way that it looked tie-dyed. *Uh-oh*, he suddenly realized. Now he was in a quandary. He glanced around the kitchen, looking for a place he could stuff the bloody dish towel out of sight. *Ahhh … there …* he thought with indemnification before the agony took over completely, and he lost consciousness.

****

Mark burst through the front door to find Meggie pacing up and down the hallway. She ran toward him as he entered.

"Thank *God* you're home! Where did you go? What did you do? I have been *sick* with worry!"

He took his wife in his arms and buried his face in her hair. He didn't want her to see that he was crying. His tears were out of a traumatic emotional release. *He could not believe what had just happened! It could have been a disaster of epic proportions if he hadn't been able to keep his cool, which he had only done by the skin of his teeth!*

"Meggie ..." he choked on his words.

His distress was terrifying her.

"*What happened?*" she cried out impatiently.

"Nothing. Nothing. Ryan is out of our lives. I don't think he'll be bothering us anymore." Mark was holding her so tightly that she thought she might break, but didn't flinch, as her mind raced with scenarios.

"Can we just go lie down for awhile? I'm not feeling too good."

"Yes, of course ... let's go." She led the way upstairs, and then curled up at Mark's side after he flopped down on the bed in an exhausted heap. She gazed at him with her cheek resting against her hands, waiting to ask the questions twirling through her mind.

They were completely startled as someone knocked forcibly on the front door. They looked at each other with fear and concern, as an unfamiliar, muffled male voice hollered out, "Mark Simpson?"

Mark extricated himself from Meggie's legs, which she had draped protectively over his, and made his way to the stairway, Meggie right behind him.

Two uniformed officers pushed their way in as Mark opened the door.

"Are you Mark Simpson?" one of them addressed Mark.

"Uh … yeah." Mark replied hesitantly.

"You are under arrest for the attempted murder of Ryan Johnson. You have the right to remain silent---"

Meggie looked on in horror.

"*Mark! What on earth have you done?*" she screeched with confused accusation. She quickly realized her mistake as she saw the pained look on Mark's face, and changed her tune before her stupidity got Mark into more trouble than he was already in.

"*Wait! What!?* No-no-no! What are you *doing*?" Meggie cried out in disbelief and shock as the two officers came into their home, and handcuffed Mark's wrists behind his back.

The cop continued, ignoring Meggie's interruption.

"Anything you say can and will be held against you in a court of law---"

"Mark! Don't let them do this to you! *Stop!* You guys have it all wrong! He didn't *do* anything! Mark! *Say something!"*

Mark was practically speechless with incapacitating panic as he realized what was happening to him.

"Please," he begged, "Officers, I didn't *do* anything. I swear. He was *fine* when I left!"

Meggie's mind was reeling. There was something … something she couldn't put her finger on. It was a … a *knowledge* – something important, but she just couldn't … *think*!

"You have the right to consult an attorney. If you cannot afford an attorney, one will be appointed to represent you before any questioning if you wish ---"

"Mark! Don't say *anything*! I'll find you a lawyer. We'll get this all cleared up – *don't worry*! It will be okay!" But her voice betrayed her doubt, and her fear that things would *never* be okay again.

"You can decide at any time to exercise these rights and not answer any questions or make any statements." The spokesman officer robotically finished his spiel.

And with that, they whisked Mark out the door, pushing his head down as they assisted him into the back of the patrol car. They drove off with lights flashing as Meggie looked absolutely helplessly on from the porch.

She didn't even know where to start. Who to call. What to do. This was a living nightmare. How could this have happened? Could Mark have tried to kill Ryan? How would he have done it? *Oh my God! Oh my God!* It was all her fault!
She never should have told Mark what happened! Some lies were necessary, and this was proof of that!
What am I going to do? she asked herself hysterically.

Meggie had no-one to call. No friends. No family. Mark was all she had – it was Meggie and Mark against the world! And Mark wasn't here to help her help him! *What on earth am I going to do?* she asked again, hoping that someone would pick her up, shake her and say, *pull yourself together, woman,* and then give her the steps to take.

Meggie found the phone book and turned to the attorney section. How could there be so many attorneys in this tiny little town? And there were so many *kinds* of attorneys! Personal injury? No. Bankruptcy? No. Workman's comp? No. Divorce? God, no! Criminal? *Really?* Was she *really* looking up criminal attorneys? She closed her eyes and dropped her finger down onto the page in the general vicinity of criminal attorneys listed. Since she didn't have a clue or recommendation, this method would work as well as any. Spiegal and Boxer. It sounded like a couple of dog's names. Boxer ... sounded like a good, fighting kind of guy. She called the number and asked for Mr. Boxer.

The receptionist quickly corrected her and said, "You mean, *Ms.* Boxer?"

Why not? thought Meggie. Women could definitely argue better than men. She was in desperate mode.

"Yes, that's right, Ms. Boxer."

Meggie was patched through to Ms. Boxer's paralegal, who took down Meggie's information, and got a very sketchy synopsis of events from the distraught wife. At this point, Meggie did not even know what had happened to them, and why they needed an attorney. But it felt good to have someone take over who knew what they were doing. Someone who could tell her what steps to take next; otherwise, she might have stumbled into a paralyzed oblivion. The paralegal assured Meggie that Ms. Boxer would go on down to the police station within the hour to talk to Mark, and advised Meggie to *stay home.*

After she hung up, Meggie was suddenly struck with that *knowledge* … that elusive thought that she had tried to conjure up when the police had been arresting Mark. It was the *knowledge* that Mark was innocent. The absolute conviction of Mark's guiltlessness and the understanding of how very capable Ryan was at *setting someone up.* She knew – she just *knew* that this was the case. *Attempted murder?* That was bad – *really bad.* But it meant that Ryan wasn't *dead!* Meggie had to find out what happened, so she ignored the advice of the paralegal, and got into her car to drive to the police station.

****

The investigators at the scene were already beginning to smell something *very fishy*. First, the neighbor who had called the police to report the gunfire was absolutely sure, he *thought* anyway, that Mark had vacated the premises prior to the gunshot. Secondly, the angle of the gunshot wound was aimed downward, and had entered Ryan's thigh from directly above. Seemed a strange place to shoot someone if your goal had been to kill, and almost at a range too close unless they were in a scuffle, which there was no evidence of. But the clincher was this: One of the investigators had arrived with a to-go cup of coffee from McDonald's. He had set it on the counter as the scene was scanned for evidence. As it sat there for an hour or so, it became cold. The officer popped the microwave door open to stick the cup in for a warm-up and *lo and behold* – discovered the bloody dish towel.

When the paramedics had arrived, bringing Ryan back around as they stabilized him, Ryan had said over and over,

"*Mark Simpson* did this! He shot me because his wife wanted to leave him for *me*. His prints are on the gun – *check it for prints!* Mark Simpson. *He* did this."

Something just wasn't ringing true about this situation. Both investigating officers could sense it. But with the victim able to identify the attacker, they had no choice but to apprehend and arrest Mark Simpson.

Ten Months Later

Mark and Meggie had never been closer. The ordeal they had been through together was like something out of some cheesy B-rated movie. It was incomprehensible to them that such a thing could have *happened to them*.

Of course, Meggie had bailed Mark out of jail right away, using up just about all of their savings. They did get their bail money returned after Mark appeared in court, which had been a joke. But not to Mark. Ironically, the cost of attorney fees had been almost as much as the bail.

Fortunately, the evidence was overwhelming as far as pointing the finger where it belonged – at Ryan. Ryan had finally confessed, with some manipulative encouragement from Meggie, who had realized all along what had happened. Had Ryan not told her the story of the priest, she might not have come to the same conclusion, though she didn't even want to *go* there. She didn't feel one iota of guilt for telling Ryan, *lying* to Ryan, that she would be there waiting for him if he would *only* confess. The fool fell for it, or maybe he simply came to the realization that the jig was up – the truth obvious.

Meggie did *not* tell Mark about what she had done. Some lies were *necessary* to tell …

Ryan was subsequently charged with several offenses, including lying to the police and filing false felony charges against Mark, the discharging of a firearm within city limits, not to mention the illegal possession of a firearm. His sentencing was still pending.

Mark and Meggie had worked successfully through any of the issues that had led them down this path of destruction, including Mark's tremendous loss, and the Christmas that had defined every Christmas to follow for the next ten years. After finally opening those historically painful presents, Mark was both relieved and chagrined to find that these gifts, innocuous and inconsequential, did not, after all, hold any power over him. They were simply every-day, ordinary items. In reality, they held no threat to his psyche, and he was even somewhat amused as he admired the outdated sweaters and sports paraphernalia that his parents had lovingly purchased for their college-aged son. The pain was still there, but he had Meggie to share that with.

The best thing that came out of all this was that Meggie was pregnant! Four months along, and happy as a clam. Speaking of clams, Mark had decided to surprise Meggie, and take her on a sort of second honeymoon to the beautiful State of Maine. His final destination was the fabled *Thunderhole*. He just never realized how final a destination that would be.

****

It was absolutely thrilling for Meggie to be back in Maine, but this time with someone who truly loved her above all else. She had always dreamed of sharing this experience with Mark, and here they were …

She had absolutely *zero* desire to look up any old haunts or ghosts, including her mother. She had managed to let it go – *completely*. Mark was grateful. He had been unsure of how a trip such as this would affect Meggie.

They were staying at an unbelievably quaint seaside hotel called *The Bar Harbor Inn*. They couldn't have chosen a more romantic spot. They ate succulent, sweet, tender, dripping-with-melted-butter lobster, right out of the ocean. They shopped the village gift stores, buying trinkets to commemorate the vacation and the renewal of their marriage … and their *lives*. They were happy. Happier than they thought possible.

On the day that they had decided to drive around Mt. Desert Island, Mark had an inexplicable uneasy feeling. He chalked it up to his concern that this trip might bring up Meggie's past in a way that would serve as a bad memory. Her excitement about the prospect of seeing *Thunderhole* again alleviated his agitation.

The day could not have been more beautiful. It was just past Labor Day, and the tourists were *gone*. They practically had the island to themselves. They made fun of the intensity of the cyclists who labored up the winding and steep hills, acting as though they were having *fun*. Mark knew better – he used to take cycling as seriously as they. He was learning that taking it easy, going at Meggie's sight-seeing pace was much more relaxing.

It was late in the afternoon when they arrived at *Thunderhole*.

Although it was early autumn, a *Spring Tide* was in effect, following a full moon and a barometric pressure that would cause such a phenomena and a significant rise in waters. The ocean's force and power was massive. Mark had never before seen anything like it, and was utterly awe-struck. Meggie delighted in her proprietary sense of "ownership" of the spectacular display.

"See? I told you it was amazing!" she called out to him over the cacophony of crashing waves.

They stood, side-by-side at the railing of the observation deck. The icy ocean overspray was both hair-raising and invigorating.

"Now I see what you mean!" shouted Mark over the din. He turned to look out over the magnificent expanse of navy-blue ocean, capped by startlingly bright and sparkling whitecaps. When he turned back around toward Meggie, she was scrambling up the side of the rocky terrain, headed toward a cliff that overhung where the amazingly high plumes of spray shot into the cerulean blue sky.

"Meggie! What are you doing!?" he exclaimed with alarm, his voice getting lost in the wind that whipped up around them.

She saw the look of concern on his face, but laughed as she carelessly shouted back,

"Don't worry! I'll be fine! I just want to see what it looks like from here!" She determinedly struggled over the edge of the ledge and sat with her legs overhanging the dangerous precipice.

Mark immediately began to climb after her, not quite believing that she could be so *stupid*. She was *pregnant*, after all!

He stopped dead in his tracks as he witnessed Mother Nature make a deciding call that would alter their lives forever.

The incredible weight of the water itself was astonishing, and took her breath away. As it furiously rained down upon Meggie in a titanic sheet, the death-grip her fingers had on

the edge of the rock was lost. She was quickly and efficiently sucked off the ledge, and her world went black.

****

Mark froze as he watched feebly while his precious wife and unborn child disappeared in the frothy white spigot of unearthly strength. His eyes attempted to follow her bright pink shirt as she was engulfed, swallowed and abducted forever by the unforgiving and selfish tide.

He wasn't sure if his eyes were playing tricks on him, but as the surge that had carried Meggie away became a receding swell as it pulled toward its center of gravity, his beloved's small white hand reached up and out of the water, almost like in a goodbye wave.

Mark slipped and slid to the granite rocks at the edge of the ocean, dropped to his knees on the cold, hard stone, and screamed,

"MEGGGIIEEEEEEEE …" The sound of his voice was completely lost.

He put his forehead against the rock and began to sob wretchedly. There was *nobody* here to help him!

NO! THIS COULD NOT BE HAPPENING! NOT AFTER ALL THEY'D BEEN THROUGH! NOT TO HIS BEAUTIFUL GIRL AND HIS YET-TO-LIVE BABY!

OH MY GOD! WHY HAVE YOU ABANDONED ME?!

Mark collapsed on the mineral-hard surface, and lay prostrate as he prayed … *begged* for God to help him.

His fervent prayers felt hollow and echoing – as if he were speaking them to an empty room.

EPILOGUE

Meggie's body was twisting, turning – churning like a pinwheel in the biting, frigid water. Here's the thing – after the initial plunge, the iciness had become merely cool, and felt good against her skin. Meggie relaxed as she was manipulated in a way that resembled an amusement ride. Her initial horror as she was pulled so forcibly off the ledge was replaced by a bewildered kind of anticipation. Anticipation of something *good*.

She was not the least bit surprised when the skinny, pale girl with curly red hair suddenly appeared at her side and took Meggie by the hand. She hadn't aged a day. Time seemed to stand still.

"It's not your time yet, Meggie. You still have work to do. Stop doing such foolish things that put you in danger." The curly haired girl spoke without a sound. Her words were just thoughts, but crystal-clear to Meggie.

Meggie had a zillion questions. Here was her chance to ask some of them! As she gazed into the eyes of her guardian angel, it was understood between them that these questions were off-limits.

The red-haired girl spoke again without actually speaking,

"I'll tell you this much. The universe is divided between good and evil, Meggie. It is a constant battle. The more that choose good over evil will be what ultimately saves us all."

Meggie listened solemnly to these unspoken words of wisdom that few would ever get to hear. Her angel went on,

"This is not all there is – not by any means. But every soul has a purpose. Do not be afraid to fulfill yours, Meggie. Try to enjoy the life you're living, and don't be afraid to face the challenges that arise. There really is a reason for everything. And somebody is always watching."

And with that she swiftly drew Meggie through the water, carrying her back to the rocky shore, gently placing her right at Mark's shivering and shaking side.

About the Author

Anne Katheryn Hawley grew up along the rocky coast of New England.

She attended Belmont College in Nashville, TN. In addition to writing novels, she is a portrait artist, fiddles around with the fiddle some, runs a Bed and Breakfast, and works part-time as a Registered Nurse. She is married and has two children and one grandchild.

She currently lives among the tall pines and crystal clear lakes of Northern Michigan.

She is the author of *Worth More Dead*, a psychological thriller about a dangerously dysfunctional family, where rivalry and jealousy between three sisters is raw and palpable. Poor judgment, impulsive decisions, and naughty behaviors result in a horrific tragedy – for which everyone pays a dear price.

Anne is currently working on a collection of eerie tales from the supernatural, to be titled *Something Wicked This Way Comes*. Date of release is scheduled for October, 2015.

Keep on the lookout for Anne Katheryn Hawley's next psychological thriller, *Killing Mom*.

Here's an excerpt:

Her heart pounded wildly in her chest. She could feel its rapid thumping in her ears. Her mouth was dry as a bone, yet her skin was broken out in a dripping, cold sweat. Her heavy breathing whistled noisily through her nostrils.

Good ... she thought, *at least my physical reaction* proves *that I have a conscience.*

The thought comforted her as she pushed 10cc of insulin, rather than the usual 10 units, into her mother's abdomen. The difference between life ... and death.

Her dear mother gazed vacantly at nothing.

Now it's just a matter of time ... Claire thought as she shakily dropped the syringe into the Sharp's container at Mom's bedside.

Claire then knelt down to pray for forgiveness for breaking at least *two* of God's commandments.